The Perpetrators

Introduction

THE PLAYERS

The end of the 2000's

The two men sat opposite each other. Roughly the same age but not a lot more in common - apart from power. In between them was a very large, old, oak desk. Mind you, these were no ordinary men - if ever you could describe such a word or a person. But, nevertheless, basically, in the history of mankind, never had such a meeting taken place between two people. But the most important point here was…….. they knew it; both of them were more than aware of their vital position in life, their social status and the major, life changing decisions they had made both for themselves and more importantly, others. Each of them was totally and utterly unique in their own way. Some would describe them as being at the top of their game. However, at the end of the day, don't we all know ourselves better than anyone else…... One of them knew he was extremely powerful, the other only thought he was and attempted to convince others of such.

The man who had been invited to this iconic office spoke first. An odd thing in itself bearing in mind their location and their positions in life but someone had to break the ice.

'Sir, you must have had time to review my proposal and I believe that is why I have been invited here. But before you give an answer may I inform you of the following, just to enforce various key points that no doubt you gathered from my report. Please excuse the plethora of figures I am about to give you but they do help clear the mist and fully explain the position,' he paused momentarily.

The other noticed his guest had not used his title. He was probably the only man in the world where such an omission was not rebuked.

'The USA Recidivism Study estimated in 1994 that within 3 years, over half of the prisoners released during that year were back in prison either because of a new crime for which they received another prison sentence or because of a technical violation of their parole. So, 68% of prisoners released in 1994 were rearrested within 3 years, an increase of the 63% found for those released in 1983.

The percentage of released prisoners rearrested within 3 years were for -
Violent crime above 60% in '83 and '84.
For Drug associated crime, plus 50% in '83 and plus 66% in '94.
Finally for Public order offences above 54% in '83 and above 62% in '94.

To put an actual relevant figure on each of those offences resulted in excess of 1/2m violent crime offences in '83 of which -
Murder numbered 8,300,
Rape 33,800,
Robbery 216,700 and
Aggravated assault 278,400.

In 1994 the total figure rose to 713,600 of which -
Murder was 9,000,
Rape 39,300,
Robbery 237,900 and
Aggravated assault 427,600.

As you can see the figures are only going one way and have been so for some time. There is no evidence at all of such figures decreasing. Now, although no one could ever think of incarcerating prisoners for life no matter what their offence or crime, the fact of the matter is, using these figures, had such existed -

In 1983 there would have been in excess of 300,000 less offences consisting of -

More than 5,000 lives saved,
More than 20,000 less rape victims,
More than 125,000 less persons robbed and
More than 165,000 less persons assaulted.

In 1994 there would have been in excess of 330,000 less offences consisting of -

More than 5,000 lives saved,
More than 20,000 less rape victims,
More than 130,000 less persons robbed and
More than 250,000 less persons assaulted.'

The guest speaking did not use notes. That impressed his host. The guest had a photographic memory for figures which had helped him greatly hence his position in life.

The guest looked at the man opposite him who had kept silent whilst he had been recounting the figures. He was sat in a very grand chair in a very grand office. Once again both totally unique. They had a history and were about to have more. These sort of men did not interrupt each other. They got where they were by listening, to the right people and, hopefully, making the right decisions.

The invited man thought about how he had arrived here. Towards the end of the 20th Century he had studied the figures in regard to recidivist crime. He studied them again and again. He had been monitoring similar figures for many years and for many reasons.

They 'hit home' on this man for very specific and personal reasons. Reasons he wished did not exist but no matter how powerful you are you cannot change the past. But unlike most people who would have read and been subsequently dismayed by such, this was no ordinary man, i.e. the type of man who would become aware of certain things and then simply forget them, move on and do nothing.

No, this was a man different to any other. He could do something about it. He knew he should do something about it. He would do something about it. After all, he was unique. But, unlike most of his fellow compatriots, this man's resolve was not fuelled by money, lust, power or control. It was fuelled by something far more powerful. That was to satisfy the needs of millions of victims who had been repeatedly let down by courts, police, barristers in fact the whole goddamn judiciary.

His mantra for many years was, 'If every living person on the face of the planet could vote on a 'specific point' how would they vote? How could they vote? How would their voices be heard? Would they want it to be heard? Would they want their choices acted upon?'

It was a virtual Taoist belief. His mantra.

But the fact of the matter was that, currently, these masses of forgotten people had no one to speak for them, no voice. They were the extremely silent majority. Politicians certainly did not seem to speak to them or for them. Military governments didn't. Royalty, Delegates, Senators, Councillors, Mayors - absolutely no one.

Up until now they had no one.
He had made a decision a long time ago. Hence his presence, now, in this office in front of this man. Despite the major decisions he had made in his life the next few minutes would eclipse all of them.

6

He intended to be the representative of the 'unheard'. The silent majority would, for the first time ever, finally have a voice.

A.

2017

United States Penitentiary Administrative Maximum Facility in Florence and colloquially known as the 'Alcatraz of the Rookies'

THE RELEASED PAEDOPHILE

The soon to be released high security prisoner walked. No, not walked, sauntered, majestically (in his sick mind's eye), slowly but reassuringly along the dreary, dim, bleached, grey concrete prison corridor. Unbeknownst to everyone, staff and inmates alike, he was relishing every moment, every majestic step, every delicious second. His determined footsteps echoed off the dull, matt walls. There was nothing soft to absorb the sound. He had hated that. No comforts, no furnishings, no curtains, no upholstery. Oh, how things were going to change for the better. He had dreamed it. He knew it. He had planned every delicious moment down to the finest detail.

His 'so called' inmates or comrades were cheering or was it jeering him on. He didn't care. Why should he? Ignorant peasants. Far more important matters were afoot. Extremely important matters. Important to him. His future now looked bright and of course, once again, it was all down to him. He was finally in control once more. His was a determined walk, confident, majestic, almost regal. King or Master of his destiny once again. Whilst they, those he was leaving behind, were still incarcerated, he was soon to be a free man once again. Free to do anything or have anything, or anyone he wanted. He was getting sexually aroused at the very thought.

18 years ago he'd been a renowned, State known businessman, for decades, earning $50m plus per annum. A big house in the Hamptons, holiday homes abroad. A top of the range red Ferrari. Famous neighbours. Regular parties. Many friends. He had it all and more. But, what was that expression - 'You never know what goes on behind closed doors' no matter how expensive those doors.

As such, not one of them had known his past nor his deepest, darkest secrets. Some might call them sordid. What would they know? He had kept his 'unusual interests' completely divorced from his everyday life. The two never coincided. He was always very careful.

'Never mix business with pleasure,' he was always saying.

In fact, in truth, there was no way he could mix business with his sordid pleasure. So life was pretty idyllic. Until it all went to Hell.

He'd waited a long time since then, 18 years incarceration to be exact, undeservedly so in his sick mind's eye. But he had used it well. Planned every detail upon his release. He was not going to make the same mistake twice. 18 years was important. Had he been released earlier he knew it may have caused a storm in the national newspapers. As it was, there was no mention of his release anywhere. No one, of interest to him, knew he was about to be released that very day. On bail, of course, but he had already worked out how to get rid of that problem. Such fitted in with his future plans. He could remain anonymous, beyond their scope.

The former businessman, now a convicted, serial child rapist, collected his items that he had handed over many years ago. The prison warder was non committal; who wouldn't be in his position when dealing with a repeat paedophile. The convict did his best to smile at the official. He could hardly contain himself but eventually he grinned. Not because he liked the warder. No, he'd finally convinced the Bail Board that he was a changed man. How easy it had been. Four, liberal do-gooders that thought they were serving the community and believed everything that he had promised. They truly believed he was a changed man. Just as well he was only convicted on the juvenile assaults and not the juvenile murders he had committed. Even he didn't think he could have talked his way out of that one.

Pity them, the fools. The Board. They obviously thought that his incarceration had taught him something. Well it had in one way. He was going to make sure he was never caught again. Perhaps he would target their children or grandchildren. He liked the irony, hell he loved the irony.

As much as he believed he was better, more intelligent than these people, there was always the nagging thought, 'How did I get caught? How could I have been so stupid.'

He knew one of his weaknesses was gullibility. He knew that he had to be careful about that in the future, his bright future; he liked saying it, 'His future.'
At last, he could now go back to his old ways and the life he once knew. He had hidden financial accounts abroad in various accounts under false names. However, this time he would be a lot more careful. He'd been planning this for many years. He could now remain totally anonymous on the World Wide Web. He could adopt a different

persona every day. They'd never catch him again. He was as free as a bird. All this dark internet stuff was not freely available or even thought of when he was an unconvicted man. What a time he was going to have. They'd made it so easy for people like him. 'Pity little children', was his sick motto.

He had been planning his first jobs upon release for the last 18 years meticulously. Most unfortunately, for him, the police had caught him as a result of a so-called friend and like-minded accomplice who had 'squealed on him' (probably upon pressure from the authorities). He was going to deal with this small matter foremost and then his former 'friend' wouldn't be able to 'squeal' any more. This time, he'd make sure he worked alone.

'If there's one thing prison teaches you,' he thought, 'It's how to commit the perfect crime!'

He was still smiling inwardly and outwardly as he stepped outside the prison gates onto a hot, sunny pavement. The sun on his face. Outside those grey walls. Free at last. Free to do anything he wanted to, have anyone he wanted . He was so happy, almost deliriously so. He felt light headed. The world was at his feet finally after 18 years. He knew he would never be in this position again. He felt giddy and exuberant at the very thought. Life was bliss.

However, although he knew he could not predict everything that was going to happen upon his release, even he could not believe what he saw in front him outside the prison gates. He looked all around him. Doing a double-take. He was the only one standing outside the gates. It had to be for him.

1.

The Supreme Court of the State of New York

THE DETECTIVE

On a dark winter's afternoon in New York, the weather did nothing to improve anyone's mood or spirits. The Supreme Court stood, dark, still and foreboding, for both defendants and those prosecuting. However, virtually every light was on. Particularly in courtroom number 1.

The court was eagerly awaiting the jury's decision in a case that was well publicised for a variety of notorious reasons. In the back of the courtroom, the seasoned, but very weary, Police Major Crime NYPD Detective sat on the hard, public wooden seats of the Court. Unlike many at the court that afternoon, he was temporarily oblivious to what was going on around him; his mind was wandering, again.

He was approaching retirement and was therefore, some would say obviously, thinking about the day he joined. He joined the Metropolitan New York Police at 18 years of age, he now had just 2 years service to go. 28 good, bad and indifferent years served. He thought of the beginning in 1989. It was funny, he thought, that when he joined, the police administration was useless even then. They had made a mistake with his DOB and recorded 15 January 1971 (15.01.71) instead of 15 November 1971 (15.11.71). This made him appear 10 months older than he was. Hence on finishing his training he was too young to go out on the streets (as you had to be 18 3/4 years old) so he had to perform security night duties on campus for 10 months!

If he didn't like the New York Training campus environment during his training he certainly didn't like it after 10 months of security night duty! Did he know at 18 years old that almost 30 years later he would be here? Did he also know that police administration would be just as bad 28 years later if not worse!

He thought about those young, innocent, fresh faced young men and women who had joined with him back then in what seemed a lifetime ago. During his time in the Anti Corruption Unit, about 6 years ago, he was able to see the records of those he had joined with. He was amazed that after 10 years service, over two thirds had left for a number of reasons (death, divorce, dismissed, etc etc). He had always felt that most of them would have made it. He did not know at this time whether that fact made him sad or not. On the one hand he remembered all their hopes, dreams and aspirations but did they all know that two thirds of them would not make to the end. It made him feel a little special but then again very sad.

Then he smiled to himself. Whilst in the Anti Corruption Unit he'd investigated his old class captain for putting $100k worth of Heroin back onto the streets. He wouldn't have voted for him then had he known what the future held. But that's probably why corrupt officers went down that road. They were never shy, retiring wallflowers. They were normally very confident, strong, bold almost psychopathic.

Albeit his mind wandered, such thoughts had entered his consciousness or even subconsciousness many times. Although they took a while to explain, the Detective could go through years in milliseconds. Was that old age, or being an old Detective that gave him that skill?

B.

THE HOE TEAM

The heavily armed teams prepared themselves. Everything had been prepped. They could and would not let their notorious, illustrious customer down. A team of four waited in a stolen van, with new number plates, at the north end of the Brooklyn Bridge. Their 5 accomplices were in a similar van on the South side. They were waiting, armed to the teeth and ready to surprise their approaching adversary in more ways than one.

Today, their customer, for want of a better word, was about to leave the Northern State Prison to return to court for final sentencing. He had been found guilty of multiple murders, conspiracy of such, kidnapping, torture, blackmail - the list was endless. He had averted justice for many years using highly paid lawyers to defeat any prosecution. Sometimes it was not the lawyers. Witnesses simply either disappeared or lost their memory! The authorities had spent years and millions of dollars investigating his affairs and fine honing their case and finally they'd got him.

As the impending incarcerated villain got into the prison van with his armed guard he looked up at the sky as if he expected some change in the weather. They pushed him roughly into the van and he sat down abruptly, handcuffed and shackled. An armed guard sat opposite him. In the guard's mind his passenger did not look as glum as he ought to look bearing in mind he was facing several life sentences. Then again, the guard also assumed you could not judge him as a normal human being. This was a true psychopath who apparently revelled in notoriety.

The prison van was led by one armed police car and behind was an armed police van. They set off on the 4 mile journey to the court.

The traffic was unusually light approaching Brooklyn Bridge. As the convoy drove onto the Bridge the first armed team drew in behind them in their stolen van as well as informing the second van of what they were doing. Upon receiving this information the second van entered the south bound traffic simultaneously. The Bridge was just over 1 mile long. The second van got to the centre of the Bridge first and violently did a ninety degree turn stopping the south bound traffic. The four man jumped out of the back of the van brandishing Kalashnikov rifles at the traffic. They surveyed nearby cars. They were looking for something or someone.

They finally spotted what they wanted - a car containing a mother and three children. To the surrounding witnesses horror two of the team dragged the mother and the children from the car and had them kneel down in front of the stationary traffic. The other two allowed and waved northbound gaping, traffic through until the armed prison arcade arrived. Anyone slowing down to take a casual gander had a Kalashnikov pointed at them. That tended to hurry them up! The police car's occupants could see what was happening and had radioed such through to their control. As they came to a halt, one of the gunmen approached the police car and banged on the window with the butt of his gun.
'Listen very carefully to what I have to say. I will say it only once. You have 30 seconds to lay down your weapons and open the back of that

prison van. If you don't, we shoot one of these,' and he pointed to the family kneeling behind him. 'The clock's ticking,' he said and pointed to his watch.

The receiving officer was a seasoned police officer. He knew when someone meant business. The officer quickly radioed the order through to his control.

Four miles away the Duty officer listened to the message as well as viewing what was happening on the bridge CCTV monitors. She knew 'help' was four minutes away. That's how long it would take to get six armed vehicles to the scene. She also knew, according to the gun men, they did not have four minutes.

One of her team spoke, 'Ma'am, we have identified the main gunman via face recognition. He has previous for this. He means business. In the past he has shot the abductees when his orders were denied.'

She could see the gunman on the monitor, looking at his watch, counting down the seconds. When he got to ten, the gunman had one of his team place the nozzle of his rifle against the mother's head who screamed even louder. 'Eight, seven, six, five, four……', said the gunman.

'All personnel, lay down your weapons. Oscar 45, inform him we will open the back of the van but it will take two minutes,' ordered the duty officer.

The officer relayed the message.

17

The gunman shouted something at his accomplices and a second gunman held his rifle nozzle to the head of the youngest child.

'Good decision commander. But, look, I know you know who I am by now. You therefore know I do my homework and get results, always. So I know you can open that door in 30 seconds, so that is what you have now got. Starting now,' and again he pointed at his watch.

The police officer had held the radio mike open so the duty officer heard every word. She was trying to buy time but it did not seem to be working. Once again the gunman counted the time down.

When he got to 3 seconds the commanding officer ordered her team to open the van. She knew it would take 2 minutes to load the prisoner and what with the heavy traffic they could stop the van at either end of the Bridge.

That's when everyone on the Bridge heard the sound of the approaching helicopter engines. As the team evacuated the prisoner out of the back of the prison van, the approaching helicopter hovered nearby. The gunman relayed a message over his radio and 8 ropes dropped down from the helicopter. Whilst seven of the team attached themselves to the ropes and one attached the prisoner, the rest of the team ran to the side of the bridge dragging the terrified mother along with them.

The main gunman shouted at the police officers, 'She's coming with us. No one follows us. If no shots are fired we will release her unharmed in due course'.

One of them grabbed the mother, they attached jump lines to the side of the bridge and abseiled into the river below. Waiting below was a powerful, inflatable rib.

The Team landed in the rib and made good their escape. The commanding police officer ordered her team to monitor the escapees but not to engage them.

Meanwhile, the team in the escaping helicopter were in high spirits. They had opened a bottle of champagne for their distinguished guest. They were all congratulating each other.

They were praising themselves so much that they did not notice the looming shadows coming up fast behind them.

2.

WANDERING MINDS

As said, the Detective's mind kept wandering. Mainly, as he often did, the Detective thought of his two friends and colleagues who had not made it (as well as all the others he had known who had died, naturally, well before their time). One was 'lost' in a riot and the other whilst working with him one night duty.

The riot situation had been whilst he was on a Sabbatical away from the Force. Had he been there, who knows. His friend, they had joined together, was the nicest and softest man he had ever met. He didn't feel as if any officer deserved what happened to him (he was hacked to death by a mob) but if ever there was one who did not deserve such, it was his friend. He had simply been in the wrong place at the wrong time. He wouldn't have said 'Boo to a Goose'.

The Detective remembered, they had water cannon at the riot. The totally ineffective Office in Charge was too afraid to use such, a political decision that cost his friend's life. Had he had the 'balls' maybe his friend would be alive today. The Detective hoped that that senior officer had sleepless nights pondering on that decision. He did not like ineffective, young, senior officers with no practical experience, at present invading the Force. There were far too many bad examples with no history of or leadership qualities (in his experience) in the modern service.

He often wondered about that other dreadful night. He had been promoted and was being shown the ropes by an older and very experienced Sergeant. One at the beginning of his supervisory years, the other at the end. They were working on a quiet sector, one apparently were you went prior to retirement, a very low crime sector. He always appreciated that, learning from older coppers who had seen a thing or two. Who had made major decisions without the aid of computers, asps, number plate detectors, videos, face fit cameras, degrees etc etc. All they had was the experience of 'investigating and detecting' crimes. He even poured scorn on his own rank. As far as he was concerned every good copper was a detective.

They had drawn the graveyard shift over the Christmas period. About 2am there had been a draw in the office to see who was working the Christmas and New Year Bank Holidays and in those days everyone wanted it for the extra money. He had got it, his older colleague hadn't and had taken the rise out of his younger partner bearing in mind his new supervisory status.

There was then a radio call to a burglar who had been disturbed but the Detective had stayed behind to assist with some juvenile prisoners after checking with his aging partner that he would be alright.

Seven minutes later his colleague had come across the suspect who ultimately cut his throat. He had also murdered his girlfriend not 3 hours earlier. Virtually every day since, the Detective had thought about those few minutes. Could he have saved his friend or would they have both been murdered? He had no high and mighty thoughts about himself. The latter was the most probable result. If 'ifs' and 'ands' were 'pots' and 'pans'.

When he had been asked to assist he was 3 seconds behind the old Sergeant. They were 2m from a corridor corner. Had he been 3 seconds ahead of himself he would have been around the corner and never heard the request to remain. 2 metres, 3 seconds which cost his colleagues life.

When he had regaled that story years later to a young rising senior officer (there seemed to be so many of them these days) he had been advised to speak to younger officers about such. The Detective had declined. A) because this was his personal baggage and not for general consumption. B) he had a distinct distrust of any advice from young, rising, inexperienced, so called star who was probably after the glory for themselves and C) at the time he had been offered zero counselling even though in todays modern police service you only had to get a papercut and the whole welfare department was on top of you. It was even worse than that at the time. As supervisors they had been told to look after the younger officers, but no one had thought about the supervisors themselves, bearing in mind it was a Sergeant that had been murdered and he was a brand new Sergeant! The deceased Sergeant had 2 years to go. Ironic. He had 2 years to go. Was it Bliss or was he just grateful he'd got here.

3.

THE DETECTIVES PAST

Then the Detective thought about his wife and young son who was six years old at the time of their deaths. He did not regret thinking about his past in this order, the fact that his wife and son had come to his thoughts after so many other things. As far as he was concerned it was all part of the natural healing process.

Initially, he did not take their deaths well at all. Who would? No amount of counselling could make up for the awful way in which they were killed, or murdered in his mind's eye. They were just in the wrong place at the wrong time and the drunken, uninsured, illegal immigrant driver failed to stop and ultimately jumped bail; he was never seen again. At the time that added to his grief, his torture. He initially thought, in his darkest moments, of trying to track the bail jumper down but even he knew he couldn't right every wrong.

After a number of counsellors he then came across one who was finally worth their salt and whom he finally appreciated. He had since been seeing her a few times over the preceding 15 years. He remembered she initially told him about a young 23 year old who had an incredible memory. He could read a book and then recite it word for word. He was in the Guinness Book of Records. The Detective at the time thought he probably never lost his keys, never forget a name, something the Detective was forever doing. Yet she explained his was not an idyllic life. The young man had attempted to take his own life 3 times before he was 21. He remembered her words, 'You see his father died and people forget that the memory is supposed to 'falter' over time. But in this young man that didn't happen and every day of his preceding life, it was as if his father had died the day before.'

It was then that the Detective realised that the human body and mind is a wonderful thing. Although he had not forgotten about his wife and son, the hurt had all but vanished. Something that never happened with the 21 year old. He even likened this belief to his and others understanding as to why there weren't more vigilantes, or grieving parents waiting at the prison steps with a loaded shotgun. Time truly was a great healer and as said, although he never forgot what happened that fateful night, the heartfelt heaviness had almost faded away.

But he knew in his own way it had affected him. He had never been able to have another relationship after losing what to him, was his soulmate, the only woman in the whole world that he could truly love. Initially, he had tried as who knows what one truly feels after the loss of a loved one. But in the end, he knew he was kidding himself. He was going through the motions but without any feelings and he knew he wasn't being truthful or honest to either himself or the women involved.

Despite the sordid world that only police officers truly know, at heart, he was a good man, an honest man. He decided that a bachelor life was not that bad. His love for his wife and his son, during those few years, were more than a lot of men experienced in a lifetime.

Additionally he felt that to have more children would simply keep reminding him of the six year old that he had lost. So taking everything into account, he had thrown himself into his job and although he had not been rewarded rank wise (mind you looking at those who were rising through the ranks this didn't worry him) he was a very well respected officer and certainly his juniors looked up to him. As far as he was concerned you could not put a price on that. There were always other ways to be a fatherly figure.

He had been a father to one whom he could not save. But during his service he had been a father figure to many, saving marriages, relationships, careers etc etc. That made him feel a lot better about his 'reson d'etre'.

C.

Arizona Open Air Prison

THE ESCAPEE

The convicted multiple murderer had bided his time well. After all, time was all he had these days; eight years worth of time to be exact. But now, it was his time. He had finally gained their confidence. After all, he'd been given 20 years imprisonment for a bungled burglary where the fucking husband and wife (and their 12 year old son) had tried to stop him. Fucking flaming, left wing do-gooders. Why didn't they take the police's advise in these circumstances? For example, 'Don't take on criminals,' he thought. Well he'd taught them a lesson and sorted them out 'good and proper' but as is often the case, he had been sloppy and been caught by leaving his traceable DNA at the scene.

But prison had taught him one thing. He now knew the system. Knew how to play it. That's what prisons had taught him and many of his compadres despite society's efforts to convert them. He'd only done 8 years, but kept his head low and now the morons had put him in a cushy open prison. The Fools.

They deserved what he was about to do.' Who the hell puts a three times aggravated burglary murderer in an open prison?' he often thought.

Mind you he had to wait. Being sloppy had got him into this mess in the first place. That was another thing he had learnt. He wasn't going to make any more mistakes. He wasn't going to mess this one up. He had just waited for the right moment and the right time and it had finally come. He had been monitoring the whole prison site for some time. The buildings, fences, lights, guards movements and timings etc etc. He had made mental notes of times, shift changes, patrol routes etc etc.

So on this particular day, on excercise duty he recognised that his best chance was where the fence was at its lowest next to the Governor's residence (probably to give the Governor a better view of the countryside).

'How ironic,' he thought.

He looked around. There were only two unarmed guards and they were chatting and looking in the opposite direction. This was it. After 8 years worth of waiting and planning. He moved quickly but not too fast so as to raise the guards attention. He knew that one jump and body roll would take him over a mound and out of sight of the guards. Within five seconds he was over the low fence and on the run.

Two hours later, he was not absolutely sure, but he felt as if he must have run for miles, continually criss crossing the river and rolling in mud so any dogs would lose the scent. Getting rid of his prison uniform for some civil clothing he stole from a clothes line. He kept checking that he wasn't being followed. Occasionally going back over his own tracks and taking a different route. This was so easy. Too easy. He got more confident the further he went. The more crossings he made, the safer he felt. 'No one could follow me, no one,' he thought.

At last, about 6 hours into his escape, he reached a dark and empty farm house in the middle of nowhere. He waited outside the perimeter for a good 30 minutes to make sure it was vacant and to make sure he hadn't been followed. After that breaking in was child's play. Although if there had been anyone there he would have dealt with them in his own 'sick' way. He had far too much to lose now. Nothing was going to stop him. He walked around the house, majestically, as if he owned the place. He noticed several photos of the family on the mantelpiece. Nice looking daughter. He might wait until they returned.

He had the best meal he'd had in eight years from their fridge and larder and a bottle of fine red wine from their wine cabinet. After booby trapping the house in case the family returned, he then settled himself down for the night looking forward to his future. A nice comfortable bed. He couldn't believe it was so easy and he promised himself he would never spend another second incarcerated.

What with the miles he had covered, the large meal and wine and the comfortable bed he was soon sound asleep. He slept well for the first time in years. He didn't even hear the ex SAS six strong team, dressed all in black, enter the house quietly at 4am easily overcoming the amateurish booby traps.

4.

THE COURTS DECISION

In the oldest court in the State the Detective came to an abrupt start. The scraping of chairs, the shuffling of court papers, voices, something awoke him. The jury was being dismissed. Nothing dramatic there so he drifted again. He worried about his mind wandering; it was becoming quite frequent recently. On the one hand he considered whether he was losing it. It had been known, officers who had almost finished their service going crazy. In his 20's he had lost his father to Motor Neurone and he often fretted that that terrible disease was hereditary. On the other hand (and to be honest, these were his true, heartfelt feelings) he thought that he been sat there, in similar circumstances hundreds of times before. He knew the system, the people involved, the rhetoric and the whole damned criminal procedure backwards. To him it was boring and very often did not always get the right result. He often asked himself whether he agreed with the judicial process when he saw another guilty perpetrator walk free. He might not agree with the process, but he knew it parrot fashion. He didn't need to be fully awake. He could do it all on autopilot.

He looked around vaguely and begrudgingly and tried to stifle a yawn. There it all was. No surprises. Same old court, same tired oak wood, same damned hard benches. Or did he now prefer comfy settees. The court even smelt the same. He was convinced that the Judge was the same one from 28 years ago. Certainly her wig looked older than him. There was the same young, aspiring, fresh as a daisy, graduate, prosecutor. Same rugged, old war horse, defending brief and as always the inevitable same decrepit, sub-human defendant, the perpetrator.

Many years ago, having dealt with his umpteenth murderer, paedophile, terrorist, child kidnapper, low life degenerate etc he had decided that such criminals had denied themselves for ever the right of being dealt with as a normal human being again. In regard to their name, he was convinced a goodly proportion of them committed a crime to get their name in the papers and on the news to achieve notoriety. So, although he couldn't delete their very existence, he had decided they had no right to keep their given name. So ever since then he had simply, personally referred to them as the criminal, defendant or his favourite word for them, 'perpetrator' or 'perp' for short.

He looked at the 'perp'. Same old sad story. Some rich guy's granddaughter had been kidnapped. The grandfather was going along with their demands but then, against the kidnappers wishes, the Police had become involved. He could not remember why, but that was certainly where he had personally become involved and why he was sitting here. The money drop was arranged but things had gone amiss. However the good news was the 'perp' had been arrested. The Detective had always thought that there were two involved and the one they arrested was the mere brawn, the muscle; the 'brains' had got away. This guy was too stupid to wipe his own arse let alone arrange a kidnapping. The 'perp' had never given up his colleague and it was felt that the young girl was murdered very soon after the kidnapping. Her body had never been found, so as is often the case, they were therefore throwing the book at the perp.

In a normal kidnapping circumstance (if ever there is such a thing) the police would have investigated the victim's family. Countless kidnappings were arranged by bankrupt, formerly rich families trying to raise some cash from kidnapping insurance policies. But this was where the case was so unique. The grandparent was allegedly the richest guy on the face of the planet and the sum asked for was a record $250m. Apparently he had raised such within minutes. It was reported that he was worth in excess of $750 billion. To him 1/4 of a billion dollars was nothing. It was chicken feed. The police had very quickly realised that there was no way the grandfather needed $250m. It was always clear that all he ever to wanted was his grand daughter back, safely.

But to be fair to him, despite his wealth and power, the grandfather had never seemed to blame the police, like so many had in similar circumstances before him. Even though the Detective had personally thought that they, the police, were ultimately responsible for the bungled investigation. No, he had gone out of his way to heap praise onto the Police and not blame them in any way. The Detective thought this was fairly unique as personally he would have been suing the Police's bungled involvement for every dime but he guessed this guy certainly didn't need the money nor the inconvenience, having just lost his only granddaughter.

The jury were re convening and the verdict was being handed to the Judge. The 'perp' was asked to stand. 'Why bother', thought the Detective, 'he's as guilty as sin'. As the guilty verdict was read out the Detective got worried. He came out of his self diagnosed autopilot abruptly. Something was wrong. Something was very wrong. The hairs on the back of his neck were standing up and he had learned, after 28 years, to trust such. They had never let him down.

5.

THE COURTROOM

As said, the Detective had been here many times before over the past 28 years. Probably more than any other officer in the Force. He knew the procedure off by heart, the rhetoric, the players, the atmosphere off pat. During his early days he spent most of his time in court. During the first two years his Sergeant wanted him to report as many cases as possible, therefore meaning that he not only attended court as a result, but he also learnt how to prepare and present evidence. A valuable lesson for later in his career.

Odd now that training had changed so much (for the worse in his mind) that officers were becoming detectives or getting promoted without ever even attending court. He remembered that recently he was asked to take a detective under his wing who had 3 years in and was due to attend court for the first time. As far as he was concerned it was far too late. What had she been doing for three years. Thoughts like this made him count the days even more so. He was tired of the modern force. It was nothing like it was years ago when he had true leaders, experienced supervision, learned colleagues. Where had it all gone wrong? It was now far more political. Senior officers making decisions to get prompted as opposed to supporting their men and women. He was so happy it could all end soon. The thought of 30 plus or even 35 years service, as they now had to do, made him shiver.

He came back to the present with a start! Something was very different this time. He had learned with experience to trust his sixth sense. It had never let him down before. So it wouldn't do now. He quickly scanned the courtroom. 'Perp' - check. Security - check. Briefs - check. Police officers - check. Sidearms - check. Judge - check. Barred windows - check. Mournful relatives or relative - check. Everything seemed alright so why was his sixth sense kicking in and the hairs on the back of his neck standing up? It all seemed okay. Everything in order. Sometimes his sixth sense was a little off kilter. But he didn't mind that. Better prepared, what was that expression - Piss poor preparation leads to piss poor performance. Was he wrong? He scanned the room again. Wrong? But no, he wasn't!

There it was. He was probably the only one to notice. He could have picked him out of a line up of one hundred, or maybe even a thousand. A slight, even, Mediterranean tan (no sign of a bottle or booth), immaculately coiffed hair, a shave that looked as though he had shaved 5 minutes ago and a suit that was probably worth more than the Detective's whole wardrobe put together. And a stance that reeked of wealth. But what was it about the millionaire grandfather sat at the back of the court? What was wrong, what disturbed him? He stared at him. Studying his every feature. By instinct his right hand instinctively covered his hand gun. Then he saw it.

The millionaire was smiling. Well maybe not smiling but there was a definite grin as he looked at the 'perp'. Stared at the perp. Up until this point he had shown nothing but remorse but here he was, at a time when most relatives would have been shouting, wailing, crying - but he was actually grinning. The Detective's analytical mind kicked in. Was there more to this than met the eye? He was willing to consider a different truth or alternatives. Such had assisted him in many cases that were going nowhere. Up until now he had assumed the grandfather 100% innocent. Could there be an alternative reason? Was he finally happy to see the perp go down? Even though the papers had been predicting such, was it the final act that drew such an emotion? But no, it didn't make sense to the Detective. There was more to it than that. It was only a slight raising of the corners of his mouth, but it seemed to mean a lot more. But what, the case was over. The verdict announced. What was he failing to see?

Then the grandfather looked directly at the Detective!

D.

THE ESCAPING RIB

The speeding rib made good its escape. It was a Technohull Sea DNA 999 with a top speed of 81 knots (93.2 mph). It had been particularly stolen due to it's twin 400 bhp outboard engines making it the fastest tender on the planet. Even if the police had followed them they could never have kept up with the 10.3 meter deep V hull. So many cop films see meagre powered police cars keeping up with escaping Ferraris and Lamborghinis. But this was the real world and nothing kept up with a Technohull Sea DNA 999. The escape team travelled three miles up the river, which took seconds, continually checking to see if they were being followed. When they were convinced they weren't they turned left sharply into what appeared to be a deserted boat shed.

The leader looked ahead into the boat shed and smiled to himself. Everything was going according to plan. This operation had been meticulously planned. They were being very well paid. So, there waiting for them was their second mode of get-away transport. A vehicle that never got stopped in New York. As they exited the rib and approached the City bus, the doors opened. The main gunman entered first, intent on congratulating the driver accomplice, on being on time. A key part of any criminal activity. However, what he did encounter was an unknown male brandishing a Koch MP5K machine gun, pointing at the centre of his head, two feet away. He recognised it immediately and knew anyone brandishing such a weapon meant business.

As he had expected his accomplice to be the driver his firearm was still in it's holster.

The unknown Koch carrying Commander spoke, 'Unless your reactions are faster than a speeding bullet, don't do anything rash.'

The villain noticed out of the corner of his eye, several other armed personnel, all dressed in black like the unknown male, covering the rest of his team and the mother with Ceska Zbrojovka Scorpion EV03s. He knew his guns and was instantly aware that any team handling such weapons were not be undermined.

The Commander exited the bus, covering the villain at all times with his firearm, never taking his eyes off him and said, 'Please step away from the rest of your team,' and he motioned with the nozzle of his Koch were he wanted him to stand.

'Here's an offer you ought not to resist,' he said to the rest of the escape team still watching their leader. 'Drop all your weapons, get in that bus and disappear. The keys are in the ignition. I won't ask you again. It's a one time offer ending in 10 seconds.'

His words were short and curt. He obviously wanted to get the information over as quickly as possible with no room for error or misunderstanding.

There was no misunderstanding. The team knew exactly what he meant as much as their leader had. They had also noticed the weapons pointing at them and knew that the assailants meant business. Each one of them looked at each other and then at their leader.

'Don't worry about your man here.' They noticed he said this without taking his eyes off their leader. He had assumed they would. He continued, 'He will not be bothering you……..' He waited a few poignant seconds and then said slightly louder, 'Ever.'

As the four man escape team, in unison, dropped their weapons and made for the bus two of the Commanders team covered them with their firearms. The other two took the woman aside and the female operative whispered quietly in her ear, 'Don't worry. We are the good guys. Your ordeal is about to end and we will unite you with your children within the next 30 minutes. You are safe now, very safe.'

The woman started to cry. Her ordeal was over. For another it had just begun.

The commander continued looking at the villain whilst a member of his team searched him for weapons, aids to escape, indeed anything of note.

'However, you, well your past appears to have caught up with you finally. So we, as it were, the judge and jury, will be dealing with the crime you have just committed as well as all your past escapades and misdemeanours were hostages have not been as lucky as this one.'

With that one of the team members searching him raised his weapon and used the butt of his gun to knock out the totally befuddled escape team leader and as he hit the ground little did he know what lay before him.

6.

THE MULTI BILLIONAIRE

The Detective was thinking about the multi millionaire and his behaviour 45 minutes later when he was making his way out of the court, down the corridor towards the exit. The grandfather's expression did not make sense. Had he truly got it wrong? He did not like unanswered questions. He was too good a Detective for that.

Suddenly he felt a tap on his shoulder.

'Here we go again,' he thought. When you've got 20 plus years in, there is always someone in police environments who recognises you, good and bad. With his memory failing him, sometimes it was more a matter of whether or not he would recognise them. Only last week a young female officer felt insulted that he couldn't remember her.

'Just wait until you've got decades of years in,' he thought.

However when he turned round it was the last person in the world he would have expected. The multi millionaire was standing there.

The grandfather spoke, 'Detective, I know you are probably very busy, but, if you could spare me 15 minutes I would like very much to explain something.'

Now the Detective's mind was going at a million miles per hour. He tried to hide his astonishment. 15 minutes to this guy was probably worth a month of his wages. But if this guy wanted to spend a quarter of an hour of his time with him then it must be important. The next sentence from the billionaire sealed it.

'But instead of being disturbed here, I am a member of a little club just around the corner - if of course you don't mind? I know you are still on duty?' the millionaire added.

Now the Detective knew this club. Hell, everyone in New York or even the USA knew this club. In New York you had 1 Oak on 453 W 17th Street, the Rose Bar at 2 Lexington Avenue and the Avenue at 116 Tenth Avenue. But this club was in a totally different league. Alleged to be the most expensive club in the world. It was called quite simply the Fifty Club on account of the fact there were only 50 members. The Detective had once read that probably half of them never attended. They were just members as a demonstration of their extreme wealth and the fact that such a membership got them into a lot of other places around the globe. Although no one actually knew, and believe you me the newspapers had tried, it was rumoured that membership was a cool $5m per annum.

The Detective had read that there were 1,500 billionaires worldwide. 560 live in the USA. However there were only about 85 multi, multi billionaires hence the figure for the club. 50 was about right, particularly in the USA. To spend $5m on membership of a club you did not attend suggested serious wealth. The Detective remembered something. Recently a painting had been sold for $400m at an auction. The buyer was not known but let's face it, thought the Detective, you've got to be one of the 85 to afford that. Then the Detective came back to reality and thought that he was going to be the first and only police Detective to enter such a club and probably the first black man.

As the grandfather ushered him outside of the court he noticed him wave to a uniformed Hispanic chauffeur on the other side of the road. Not what the Detective would have thought. The driver was young and the car wasn't particularly grand. An understatement although he thought that was probably why this guy had remained under the radar for so long. He didn't know his cars but it simply looked like a stretched Volvo. The Detective instantly reminded himself that, prior to the kidnapping, the multi millionaire was hardly known. He had remained very much beyond the tabloids reach (apart from the story about the painting), despite his wealth. Try as they did, and they had tried extremely hard, they had found it impossible to dig up any dirt on the multi billionaire. They couldn't even make it up from some spurious sources like they normally did. He paid his taxes, he did not get involved in politics, no dodgy liaisons, dalliances or divorces, no errant children, no sexual deviance. Nothing on social media. Nope, he was squeaky clean and virtually unknown. That was probably why there was no bodyguard, no Rolls Royce. How the hell do you do that when, if you were a country you would be the fifth richest country on the planet? The Detective once worked out that the guy and his companies earned more in 15 seconds than he did in a year!

His immense wealth meant that the Detective (and probably most of the public) ought to have despised the guy. No one makes that much money without crossing someone. But try as he may any dealings he had had with the man up to now had resulted in him ultimately liking the guy. There did not appear to a be a bad bone in his body. He felt this impossible. He was once told that millionaires were happy to tell you how they made their fortune but they would never tell you how they made their first million as it had undoubtedly involved crossing someone or doing something illegal. Not so this guy, squeaky clean.

7.

THE FIFTY CLUB, NEW YORK

As they made their way to the entrance of the Fifty Club the Detective's mind was, as said, going at a million miles per hour. What, why, when, how? The Detective liked to think that he had been involved in or heard about every situation that could face a man or woman. He therefore felt he could predict outcomes with almost 100% accuracy. However, this was not one of them. He had never been in such a position, or anything like it, in his entire life. He as out on a limb. But he was determined that his lack of experience would not mean that he let himself down in either his profession or his very being.

No words were being spoken. It was as though the millionaire wanted to wait until they were completely alone which only added to the mystery and suspense. In order to not let such things set in, as a panic, he looked up at the monstrous building. He'd walked past it a thousand times before and never given it so much as a second glance. But this was different. He therefore studied it like he had never studied a building before. It was almost Gothic, dark and brooding, like going back in time, very old and huge. Certainly too vast for 50 members. Maybe that was the point. Since size meant wealth apparently, he understood the nature of the immense building. It reeked wealth and opulence.
He watched the footman greet the billionaire. He noticed that the footman had 'clocked' him almost 50 feet from the entrance. He

obviously assumed that footman at this sort of venue were at the top of their game. The Detective had met many footman, bouncers, whatever you wanted to call them; he had been to many venues intended for so called stars and alleged millionaires. He always felt that the staff despised these so called VIPs and probably ended up spitting in their drinks or doing untold sorts of things to their meals. However, this was different. It was more than obvious that the doorman not only knew this particular member, but also knew he could tip him a month's wages at the drop of a hat and therefore there was no resentment, no hidden anger, only complete and utter respect. The footman had learned, as had he, that there was a huge difference between millionaires, billionaires and trillionaires. If you are going to try and impress anyone then you've got to be able to spot the difference.

The doorman even knew his host by name which was probably not hard to do if there were truly only 25 regular attendees. He announced it on greeting him, but then proceeded to call him 'Sir'. But what really did impress him was fact that the millionaire knew the footman's first name and that went hand in hand with the Detective's initial thoughts; that this guy was not like your normal rich guy, if there was such a thing. It reminded the Detective of a saying he once heard and which he liked to apply to himself. And that was, 'Be kind to the people you meet on your way up, just in case you meet them on your way down.' The Detective smiled to himself. He felt that he had probably had a lot more 'downs' than the millionaire. Just to enforce his previous point - the billionaire even asked the footman about his daughter who had apparently been seriously unwell recently. He asked if the contact number he had given him had helped. The doorman nodded enthusiastically and thanked him profusely.

Whilst this was going on the Detective remembered; he had watched a programme some time ago on TV entitled 'Who wants to be a Billionaire?' The program basically sold the line that theirs was a lonely, sad life with no real friends or partners and a complete and utter disregard for the common man or woman. They did not have homes, they had acquisitions. They were psychopaths, devoid of any emotion or empathy. But the mere fact that he knew the staff's name and his other behaviour added to the Detective's original assumption. Additionally, he spoke to the Detective as if he was his equal. On top of all this he wanted to know if the system really worked. It did. He desperately tried to see what he tipped the doorman. He was convinced it was four $500 bills.

8.

THE CONVERSATION

As they entered the portals of the Fifty Club the Detective noticed another member who was being greeted ahead of them. The entrance hall was larger than the Detective's whole apartment. Their voices echoed off the huge granite portals. It was almost regal. All the Detective could see was his back and an overcoat that reeked of wealth. There was the same reverence offered to the other member by the concierge and then he was whisked away as if they did not want members to see or acknowledge each other. That went hand in hand with the 'no friends' belief. The 25 regular members probably had a room each, or rooms!

The Detective was interested as to how he would be introduced to the staff. Or if indeed there would be any introduction. Did the staff recognise that it was not up to a member to have to lower himself as to introduce a guest to a member of staff? He would have chosen the latter but for the fact that the billionaire said to the receptionist, 'This is my personal guest and he is to be treated as if he were a member.'

They were guided to a room that reeked of leather, fine wines, cigar smoke, roaring fires as big as your kitchen and oak everything. It was as if the Detective had gone back in time. There was a huge fire next to two enormous leather chairs to which they were guided. The wine waiter appeared, as if by magic. He then went onto say that he knew the billionaire was in town and he had therefore ordered his favourite wine on the off chance he may attend (well that's got to be worth a $1k tip thought the Detective). His host asked him if to was not too early for a glass of fine wine. All the Detective could think was that here was an opportunity for him to possibly taste the finest and certainly most expensive wine of his life and he was not going to give it up no matter what the time of day. He noticed that two glasses were prepared. No taster to see if everything was alright and not corked. The Detective amused himself with the thought that at these sort of establishments and prices there was no way anything purchased would be anything less than 100%, less than perfect. When the Detective took hold of the glass he almost gasped. The weight, the feel, the clarity of the glass, the cut of the design. The Detective was no expert on glassware but even he knew this was a unique experience. Not only was the wine very expensive, the glass was probably worth more than his car.

Over the next hour the millionaire talked. At first the Detective was of a mind to learn everything he could about his host. But it soon became very apparent and clear that this guy did not make his billions by giving away any secrets; anything he did impart, was only what he meant to give away. He realised it was not every day he chatted to a true billionaire. His investigative conversation and techniques were not cutting any ice with this particular man.

When the Detective thought about the conversation later he thought that the vast majority of it consisted of the billionaire telling him of his views on the judicial system and quizzing him on his own thoughts. The Detective was used to this and only gave the party line despite being pressed by his host on areas such as expensive briefs getting guilty clients off, sex perps getting away with easy treatment in mental institutions, as opposed to hard time and light sentences handed down to major criminals despite their victim's families facing a lifetime of pain. The Detective had entertained such questions many times and knew that his only response could be and ought to be the official, police and judicial system party line.

The self made billionaire knew about the Detective's view on 'perps' and the name he gave them. Hell, half the city knew since he'd let it slip a year ago to a reporter and it was spread all over the newspapers much to his seniors annoyance. That was probably another nail in his coffin in regard to promotion. He remembered his young supervisor thinking it not very PC. However his host seemed to be of an alternative mind; he seemed to very much agree with his view on the 'perp's' anonymity, for ever more.

His main thoughts centred around the time. It was getting on for 2 hours since they had entered the Club. All he could think was how much this guy could earn in 120 minutes and therefore why spend so much time with him. The final part of the conversation attempted to resolve this.

The man opposite him mentioned that he, the Detective, might have noticed him at some point during the proceedings (he did not mention the word 'grinning'). It became apparent that this oligarch actually cared about what the Detective might be thinking or may have thought of him. This once again enforced his previous positive thoughts. His host did admit to the fact that he was finally glad that the proceedings had come to an end and that he never had to look at the 'perp' looking so well, ever again. The Detective thought a lot about this. He thought these were an odd combination of words.

All of a sudden matters seemed to be coming to an end. His host asked the wine waiter to bring the rest of the crate of wine. He then went on to offer the Detective and his team the crate as a way of saying 'thank you' to his department. He had noticed the Detective seemed to enjoy the wine (who wouldn't) and he would be offended if there was a refusal. The Detective was of the mind that this was a person whom you did not refuse. His host even offered him the use of his car and chauffeur as he realised that the Detective could not carry the crate through the streets of New York. He would sort his own transport. This added to the billionaires uniqueness. How many in his position would be happy grabbing a cab or taking public transport. It reminded him that the granddaughter had attended not what you would call an Ivy League school. Her grandfather had deliberately tried to negate their wealth by hiding her away, in a 'cheaper' public school.

'How ironic,' he thought.

E.

ABOARD THE HELICOPTER

Suddenly the escaping helicopter pilot brought the attention of the celebrating team to three aircraft fast approaching them from behind. The pilot was a former Vietnam War veteran. He instantly recognised the Boeing AH-64E Apache Guardian helicopters as one of the most deadly aircraft on the planet. They are fitted with a mast mounted antenna with updated Longbow fire control radar. They could fire Hellfire 2 anti-tank guided missiles in fire-and-forget mode. Added to that they have an updated targeting, battle management system, cockpit communications, weapons and navigation system. Finally, they were each fitted with a 30mm cannon. All armed with enough firepower to take out a small town let alone their rather smaller helicopter.

Upon seeing them the recently released convict shouted at the pilot, 'Get the hell out of here.'

'You've got to be fucking kidding. I can't outrun those fuckers. One of them maybe, but not three,' shouted back the pilot.

Two of the gun ships drew alongside the smaller helicopter. Their 30mm cannons were pointing at them - directly.

Suddenly a voice came over their radio.

'Good afternoon gentlemen. You may have noticed that you are slightly out paced and out gunned as it were. Or, if you haven't by all means make a run for it. It will be my utmost pleasure and my Plan A, to blow you out of the sky,' said the voice calmly and eerily.

The transmitted voice continued, 'Or consider my Plan B. You simply follow my lead helicopter to a nearby, private, airport. All of you will have free access to leave once landed. Apart, of course, from the gentleman you have just released. He will be coming with us.'

The escapee started to shout at the pilot.

The transmitted voice continued.

'If he offers you anything to go against my plan, just consider whether or not it's worth more than your lives. I would imagine the man in question does not like my plan A or B so I would make sure, if I were you, that he is unarmed and possibly restrained, immediately.'

At this point the pilot felt a jolt through his joystick as a magnetic mine was fired from the rearmost helicopter attaching itself to the shell of the escapee helicopter.

'By the way, that bump you just felt is set to detonate in 15 minutes. The airport is 12 minutes away so best you make your decision immediately, or we simply go back to Plan A,' said the extremely authoritative voice.

All of the escape team were ex-military. They were used to making instant decisions and on seeing the three Boeings they knew there was only one way out of this predicament. With that two of the escape team jumped on the man they had just helped escape. They pinned him to the floor. One of them shouted to the others, 'What the hell are the rest of you doing? There's no way out of this. We can't possibly escape those fuckers so let's take his offer and live to fight another day.'

With that two members of the team pulled the escapees hands behind him and tethered them with plastic hand ties.

The pilot, watching all of this, noticed that his radio was tuned to the helicopter following them. He pressed his transmit button, 'Looks as though we are going with plan B. Show us to the airport.'

'Very wise decision,' came back the reply.

One of the helicopters beside them took up a position in front of them. The pilot noticed all of its firepower was pointing towards the far smaller helicopter.

The pilot dutifully followed.

9.

THE CHAUFFEUR DRIVEN RIDE TO THE POLICE STATION

Very soon after he exited the Club the Detective found himself at the boot of the Volvo as the chauffeur loaded the crate of wine. Not many words had been spoken but the Detective thought, albeit a 15 minute journey, that he was determined to find out a little more about the billionaire via his chauffeur. He kind of guessed the chauffeur wouldn't be as guarded as his boss so surely it would be easier for him to elicit a little information than from the billionaire. After all he was a Detective.

The driver seemed quite chatty at first. He was willing to talk and when questioned he explained, 'Yeah man, the previous chauffeur was using the limo for private work and other kinds of stuff. The Boss is really big on trust and stuff and there's no way he was going to have a chauffeur who lied to him. Sacked him on the spot. Even drove the limo himself for a few days. Can you imagine that. Drove his own fucking car. Anyhow, my mum is one of the Boss's cooks - you know he's got 4 of them and she mentioned to him that I was a good driver.'

The Detective subtly questioned the chauffeur about this special part of the conversation.

'Yeah, alright man, yeah. My life was going down the pan. I needed a good stable job with a good Boss and of course mothers are always looking out for their sons aren't they? Mind you she told me, if I let the her down then she was letting the Boss down and if he didn't kill me, she would!' He then let out a raucous laugh. The Detective could well imagine the conversation.

The Boss has given him a three month trial which he had passed with flying colours. The Detective tried a few more searching questions but the chauffeur had 'shut up shop'. At this point the Detective realised that he was never going to get any more from this guy. He was never going to roll over on a man that had given him a new lease of life. As his Boss had trusted him, he was never going to sell that trust by revealing anything to a police officer. He did however wonder whether the chauffeur had kept quiet of his own volition or whether his Boss had 'prepped' him prior to the journey. He couldn't really guess either way.

The 15 minute journey went very fast. He did however take the chance to look around the car. 'Maybe,' he thought, 'It looks plain on the outside but inside.......' But no, it was just as plain and mundane on the inside. A few extras but no chilled bottle of champagne, no disco lights, no sheepskin carpets or seat covers. Yes, it reeked of leather but then again so did most cars these days he surmised. It was at this point the Detective thought, 'What does a guy with that amount of money spend it on apart from expensive clubs and wines?'

At the end of it the Detective realised he had learnt nothing new. Well nothing particularly new about the billionaire. Although the story about him taking on the young chauffeur did tend to reaffirm his belief that amazingly, he seemed one of the, very few, good guys, despite his vast wealth.

At the end of the journey the Detective's only thought did not relate to the billionaire or the chauffeur. It was how the hell he was going to get an expensive crate of wine into his office without anyone seeing him.

10.

THE WINE

Later that day the Detective sat at his desk in his office.

He was daydreaming, again.

He came to but never regretted his little 'power naps'. He had been dropped off 'round the corner' as he did not want to be deposited by the limo right outside the police station and walk in with a crate full of of wine. Not the done thing as it were. So he had taken a rear entrance and stairway and now sat at his desk looking at one of the bottles he had taken out of the crate and placed on his desk. He didn't even know the name but he did know it tasted very nice. He had always wondered about expensive wine. Was it worth the money?' He had kidded himself it wasn't but that idea had just been blown out of the water. The wine was obviously expensive and definitely in a different league to his normal $19 bottle from his local supermarket.

He was also considering the last few hours. None of it really made sense. The length of time spent, the location, the unusual conversation, the need for solitude. One thing he had learnt during his career. The Detective liked putting criminal jigsaws together. He pondered, finding, placing and moving pieces of the jigsaw. This process had helped him many times. Those words used by the millionaire regarding the perp. 'Never see the perp again looking so well'. Why did he ever think he would see the perp again, whatever he looked like? This 'jigsaw' definitely had a few pieces missing.

At that point his door swung open and the youngest recruit to his department entered. The Detective didn't like the fact that he didn't knock and would have mentioned it. He was a young flyer and apparently very intelligent and educated and highly thought of. The Detective had taken him under his wing just as someone had done for him all those years ago. Whatever he came in for, and the fact that he was going to remonstrate with him for his sudden entry, went right out of the window as soon as the young sprog spotted and latched onto the bottle of wine on the desk. He picked it up and read the label. There was silence for a few seconds. He then uttered several expletives.

'Blimey Sarge, how the hell can you afford a bottle of wine like this? In fact where on earth did you find it?' asked the young recruit.

Something very quickly dawned upon the Detective as the young DC typed away on his mobile phone murmuring words like rarity, unique, one off, never seen it before in the flesh. He then let out a few expletives and said, 'Blimey, it's worth at least $6,500!'

As the Detective very quickly worked out that there was a further $78k worth of wine under his desk he leaned forward and casually pushed the case with his foot a little further under his desk so it was out of view. He was quickly working out that things did not look good. There was no way he could accept a $78k gratuity. Questions would be asked, investigations would take place. Particularly by micro managing busy bodies. His mind was turbo charged. It then dawned upon him that this young whipper snapper obviously knew a thing or two; about the bottle of wine and it's rarity and was therefore probably a bit of a wine snob. He felt he could use this fact to save his skin.

He thought very quickly and then explained to his younger protege, 'Well the fact is I've actually been given 2 bottles by the kidnapped victims grandfather.'

He waited for this to sink in and then added, 'You know to share such a fine wine with those guys out there and the fact that he had just been given 2 bottles. Well I feel that to share such amongst them bearing in mind they wouldn't know a Merlot from a Cabernet. Wouldn't it be far better idea for me to have one and you have the other as you more than obviously appreciate a good bottle of wine and I would guess that at $6.5k a pop that this is a seriously good wine?'

Out of respect for his mother he kept his fingers crossed under the desk all the time he was talking.

'Of course this means that we ought to keep this to ourselves,' he added.

He knew that for the youngster to brag about such would mean that he did not get a chance to taste a $6.5k bottle of wine and therefore anonymity was guaranteed. The young DC assured him, 'Errrr, yes Sarge. If you think that's best then who am I to disagree. Yes, I can guarantee I will not breathe a word of this and thank you for the opportunity as I don't think I will ever be able to afford a bottle like that in my life.'

He backed out of the office still thanking the Detective and swearing anonymity with the bottle very firmly hidden under his jacket. He seemed to handle it as if it were a small Improvised Explosive Device. As he shut the door the Detective smiled to himself.

The Detective then quickly and desperately thought about the other 11 bottles lurking under his desk. For a moment he was very worried. But then decided that he had never done anything illegal, never stolen anything during his career, he had always been honest, above board, uncorrupt. But! He had also never been praised for all the positive things he had achieved in his profession, had been passed over for inexperienced officers just because they had a degree or knew someone, had been maligned because his face (or pigment of his skin) did not fit. He remembered his time in the Anti-Corruption Unit investigating officers for putting $100k worth of heroin back onto the streets, for stealing half the drug sellers wares and then putting the stolen drugs back into circulation. These were corrupt officers. Although he did remember a time a senior officer officially reported him as he had made a mistake on his duty states. At the time his mother had been very ill and a good friend had cancer. His mind was not on anything let alone an administration procedure. No one had believed him. That was without doubt the worst supervisor he had ever come across. A total micro manager and not a leader. One colleague described him as not being worthy of driving an early turn prisoner van. As far as he was concerned that put down van drivers. Roll on 24 months.

He thought about his two former colleagues looking down on him as he often did in times of concern. What would they think? He looked up at the ceiling and promised himself that each Christmas Eve, upon his retirement, he would open up a bottle and drink to his fallen comrades.

He smiled to himself. He could see them smiling down on him. He knew he would sleep easy with such a decision and not rattle too many heavenly cages.

His mind drifted again.

He had another thought at a recent Old School Boys reunion. He had not attended one for years. He had always felt that he had undersold himself a little as a New York Detective. He guessed that most of them would be bankers, self made businessman, stock brokers etc etc. However, during an evening meal he was chatting to a table full of old school boys; it turned out he was the only one who had 20 odd years in the same career. For all those years he thought that they had done better than he had. What a waste. He walked a little taller that night.

His thoughts then went onto his forthcoming retirement; time was going by so fast. He'd been told it got faster the nearer you got to the end but no one ever believed it. However it was true. The last 2 years had gone by in the blink of an eye. He recently told his mother he had 2 years to go. She was convinced he had said, only last week, that he had 4 years to go. He delighted in telling officers with 5 years left that it would fly by. He knew they didn't believe him which made him chuckle as he knew they would be saying the same thing in a few years.

His mind kept wandering despite what was going on around him. Thoughts - intentions, dreams (the dreams of thousands of police officers that had gone before him, probably all over the world); his dreams - the small beach house, the sound and feel of the sea, a one-man row boat, sea fishing, an open top sports car, living miles away from anyone, from anywhere - particularly this courtroom and city - utter bliss after years of turmoil.

He thought back to when he joined. In the police canteen you had the probationers table, the drivers table, the detectives table and then the 'soon to be retired' table. Woe betide you if you sat at the wrong table. On the odd occasion that he had heard the conversation at the 'retired' table it centred around the thoughts he was now having . He could not believe that time had gone by so fast nor that the 'conversation' had not changed in all those years. However, despite everything, despite the good and the bad, he was grateful he had got to this point for several, sombre reasons.

The Detective's daydreaming continued.

During, what he considered, his illustrious career he had been shot, stabbed, run over and beaten up so many times he had lost count. His body and more importantly, his heart and mind, showed the battle scars of all those years. He'd made the same mistake that probably all coppers made and probably all employees. They presumed that they would retire in the same state of health as when they started their employment. Yet here he was - a bout of kidney stones (that he swore caused more pain than the stabbing), suffering from sciatica, probably only a few years away from a new hip and a numb feeling in his left foot that the experts were still deliberating about. He grinned to himself. The open top sports car he had promised himself on retirement, had originally been a Harley Davidson motorcycle but his bad back had put paid to that.

The 'shooting' was when he was 19, a rookie cop. Not as serious as it might sound. He didn't even know he had been shot! His HOE Team were getting changed after completing a late turn when a bullet fell from his anorak on to the concrete floor. He chuckled to himself; in those days there was no such thing as bullet proof vests. But there was such a thing as wearing your pyjamas under your uniform both for warmth and the fact that the police shirts and trousers were so coarse they irritated your skin. So basically, as it was winter, he'd been wearing a normal vest, his pyjamas, a shirt, a jumper, his tunic and an anorak and that is what had saved him as this 'stray' bullet could not even penetrate six items of clothing! He thought to himself that too many people believed cop films where a handgun shoots a person half a mile away. Most handguns weren't very powerful and just as well for him. He often thought that he hoped it was a stray bullet as opposed to someone taking a potshot at him.

But the funniest thing was the way his colleagues treated it back then. Were they shocked, amazed, thoughtful, considerate? No! No chance. Police humour is far too brutal. What did they do at this dire time that could have been fatal? They laughed their socks off and once they finished ribbing him they picked up the bullet and threw it in the bin. That earned him the nickname Bullit for 5 years! How different it would be today. Forensics, investigations, ballistic tests, counselling. How times have changed, he mused. But were they any better?

The stabbing was a little more serious. He had learnt at first hand, (he liked the pun), that you do not try and disarm someone on crystal meths, armed with a knife with nothing but your own two hands. In your first two years you tend to think you are bulletproof. He often looked at the scar on his left hand to remind himself how lucky he was. He also showed such to as many rookies as possible so they would learn by his mistake and not at first hand. He thought about his early days. Night duty, on the beat, no radio, no firearm, no asp, no handcuffs and yet he would stop anyone he thought necessary. He reported his first burglary over a pay phone! Today he felt that he wouldn't stop a random vehicle without an armed unit, a dogs teams and a Support unit behind him. He had a great deal of admiration for younger officers from that point of view. He pondered, do you get wiser as you grow older, or scared?

Lastly the 'being run over' or 'attempted murder' as far as he was concerned. He and his partner had disturbed two burglars one night duty in the early hours. One of them tried to escape in a stolen car. The car was in a very narrow alley and as he approached it, the burglar jumped in the driver's seat and gunned the engine. There was nowhere for him to go, no alleys, no side turnings, no doorways, nothing - so he literally ran for his life. As he got to the end of the alley he desperately dived left, for his life. He could hear the engine right behind him, just as the stolen car brushed past and crashed into the wall opposite. That is why he thought the charge should have always been attempted murder as there was no way on heaven and earth that the driver was attempting to turn left or right at the end of the alley and escape. His sole and utter intention was to run the detective down. He turned out to be an 20 year old student on holiday who'd met up with the wrong kind. Mind you the Detective never thought him that innocent as he had steadfastly refused to give up his partner!

Then, months later, at court, the burglar's mother accosted him saying he was persecuting her son and ruining his life. Me, he thought, not the low life who recruited her son. He remembered feeling, momentarily, a little pity for her but then he remembered how her son had tried to kill him so he let her have both barrels (verbally) in the court corridor. He never felt bad about that, even though she was reduced to tears, as he knew, in his job, a few milliseconds, a few inches could mean death and once again he was very lucky in that alley. But he always liked to think his glass was half full. The burglars had nicked a low powered Hyundai. He felt that if they nicked a faster car he might not have made it to the end of the alley!

F.

TICONDEROGA AIRFIELD

Upon approaching Ticonderoga air field the escape helicopter was guided to a landing pad at the north end of the disused airfield.

Upon landing they were greeted by a dozen heavily gun toting personnel.

The landing crew signified for the pilot to kill his engines. Once it was reasonably quiet one of the greeting crew spoke over a loud hailer.

'Please, all of you leave your weapons in the helicopter and then make your way to the black bus at the north end of the airfield. Also, please leave your tethered 'customer' on the helicopter, face down.'

The team heard every word, looked at each other, looked at the at the heavily armed personnel outside and at their restrained escapee. They had all quickly worked out that they were not the intended targets for this mission. The 'target' had always been the person currently restrained on the floor of the helicopter. Their decision was already made. They all nodded to each other, left their weapons on the helicopter and vacated.

Once the escape team had made good their own escape (followed by two motorbikes - part of the greeting team to make sure that they did actually vacate the scene) the commanding officer entered the helicopter, sat down and leaned down so she could talk to the escapee. Whilst he did so a colleague checked that the 'prisoner' was sufficiently restrained. Another of her team disarmed the mine attached to the helicopter.

'Well then, I have some good news and I have some bad news for you. First the good news. Congratulations, you have escaped and you will not be imprisoned or sentenced by the State later this afternoon or any other day for that matter. So the $5m you paid for your escape has been well spent. From that point of view you sort of achieved your aim. However, now the bad news. Dependant on which way you want to look at it. Some of your victims may consider this the good news. Well, the bad news is that both you and the lead team member who planned this little escape will become 'guests', as it were, of our Boss.'

'All will be explained once we get to our venue and please do not waste your time thinking of planning an escape. No one knows you are here or more importantly where you're going and I guarantee, no one cares. Actually, in time you are going to wish you never escaped.'

With that two team members entered the cockpit. The grabbed hold of the escapee and loaded him into a van that had reversed up to the helicopter.

In 2 hours they would rendezvous with other members of their team who were transporting the lead member of the escape team. Then both men would make their journey, their final journey, together.

11.

THE DETECTIVE'S LIFE

Over the next few months nothing really changed in the Detective's life either personally or vocationally. He had attended a number of meetings for about-to-be retired officers, some good, some bad. Some he thought he should have attended a while ago as their advice was too late. But in himself he felt assured about his future plans. One thing he wanted to achieve was, no regrets.

The 'wine' problem had died a death in that nothing had been mentioned by anyone, not even a hint of such. With every day that passed were expensive wine was not discussed, the more he looked forward to honouring his fallen colleagues, in his own way, over the next few years. He had never felt guilty about this. In actual fact, he was looking forward to it. He had thought a lot about his fallen comrades. About the fact that they would never got the chance to celebrate their retirement or enjoy it. He took it upon himself to honour them by always trying to be positive and the faster he was approaching his retirement the more positive he was becoming.

He had had many highs and lows during his career. But one thing he prided himself was that in the main, all those who served under him, tended to appreciate him. He liked that. Not so at present with his two senior officers. It was if they despised the fact that he was retiring before them. They chose every opportunity to undermine him on the smallest of matters. Micromanaging to an extreme. He wondered sometimes whether they were right and he was wrong but so many officers came to him and supported his views that he thought he must be right. 'Maybe it is better this way,' he thought. 'Finishing on a low makes you appreciate your retirement even more so. He would have hated to leave on a high and then miss such as he ventured forth into retirement. Far better this way. It also made him better at dealing with his two protagonists.

He tried not to think of them. Better thinking of more positive things or at least better officers.

Only last week another officer had been murdered. He was attempting to put out a Nail Chain to stop a stolen pick-up truck. The 18 year old driver just mounted the central reservation and mowed down the traffic officer. The officer didn't stand a chance. The Detective felt that his was the only profession (outside the military) were employees or their families didn't know whether they were coming home that night. A week later the 18 year old was caught. Apparently, he had said 'Sorry'. That was really going to bring the officer back, wasn't it! What an 'empty' word after causing the death of another. It was quite simply murder yet in his heart of hearts the Detective knew he would be charged with a menial traffic offence. He often thought, if a murderer truly wanted to get away with killing their wife, husband, boss etc etc then just run over them. 5 years at the most compared to life was a far better deal. Not that he went around preaching such.

As the days passed by, he thought about his wife and son. How they should have been there to celebrate this part of his life with him. He imagined both of them planning for his retirement. Presents, cards, signs, vacations, whispered conversations. As quickly as he thought about such, he quickly forgot about it. Such thoughts did him no good. Concentrate on the present and secondly the future was what his counselor used to say. So he was determined to make the most of everything. His dear mother was going to be heavily involved in his retirement. He was going to make sure that she enjoyed it as much as he was going to,

His retirement was getting closer. He could almost smell the sea. He'd attended a few seminars intended for those about to retire. Their basic premise, was - invest one third long term, invest one third short term and the other third. Well, remember them talking about the light at the end of the tunnel. No, it's not an oncoming train. Your rainy day has arrived, go out and spend a third on whatever your little heart desires! After all, tomorrow, you might get run over by a bus. What's the use of being the richest man in the graveyard?

He liked this idea of three thirds. One third on the beach house (long term), one third on stocks and shares (short term) and one third on his beloved boat. Spend every day as if it were your last. No more shifts, no more armed sieges, no more courts or perhaps, no more of all the negative police and public shit. No more 'perps'. Bliss.

Amazingly he had bumped into MB a few times; he had given the millionaire this title (Multi Billionaire) and MB had liked it (however the irony was the Detective had now decided MB was probably a Trillionaire). He met him a few times, funnily enough purely by chance. No matter how many meetings the conversation had always been the same. Therefore he thought nothing of it. He felt like it was a game where MB was trying to get out of him his own personal thoughts on these subjects. The harder MB tried, the more resolute the Detective became.

All that changed 18 months from his retirement.

12.

BAD NEWS

One bitter, cold, winter evening the Detective visited his mother, as he did every Monday. He became suspicious as he approached her apartment as all the lights were out but he knew she was home. He used his own key and quickly realised no crime was involved. He flicked on a light switch and found his mother crying, desperate, alone in a darkened kitchen. She was still in her night dress from that morning. She hadn't eaten all day. She hadn't washed. She looked frailer than he had ever seen her before. He felt powerless. His heart bled. He gently and sympathetically put his arms around his mother and asked her what had happened. It took a while for his mother to explain. Turned out his 18 year old niece was on a life support system at the local Hospital but things did not look good.

The poor girl had led a continuously, troubled life, despite the Detective mentoring her and trying to look after her in the absence of any other male, role model. But, as is often the case, she had fallen in with the wrong sorts, or rather been sucked in like so many kids on the streets devoid of friends and family. He remembered a figure from when he was a custody sergeant in one of the wards. He had booked in in excess of one thousand youths under 17. In only one case did both parents turn up. In the majority of cases it was either a single parent, another relative but more often than not someone from the social services. That said he never condoned single parent families. He knew that most of them were working double shifts to make ends meet. He didn't despise them, he praised them. But what chance did kids stand when locally 25% came from families with both parents, 25% with one parent, another 25% lived with another family member and the remaining 25% didn't live with any relative at all. For them the gangs became their family and they expected the police to put this right. When the real problem probably started the day they were born. What chance did they stand?

So the cause of his niece's problems. Well the latest finest example conjured, manipulated and helped develop her drugs habit, in order to farm her and her body out. Regular beatings and offers of drugs kept her in line. Any action he tried to take against the 'perp' resulted in his niece hating him. He therefore, rightly or wrongly, backed off.

However, over the past month, she had threatened to leave this part of her life (after a few harsh words from her Uncle, who knows?) But then this. Was it a drugs overdose or did her pimp deliberately give her the wrong mix? Either way, as far as the Detective was concerned, the pimp was 100% responsible. The Detective knew this wasn't the pimp's first time. He knew he should have got his niece out earlier. His mother had never had a daughter and hence he had never had a sister. In a way this young girl had filled that void and now some low life had taken it all away from them. Despite all his 'power' he could do nothing for the situation or more importantly, his mother. He did the only thing he could do. He stayed with his mother that night and consoled her.

G.

THE KIDNAPPER

The sultry, lone figure was waiting, alone, apart from his victim in the bedroom next door. He smirked to himself as he always did when he was in this position. Never caught, always free. It had been and was the perfect crime. Well, if you are going to kidnap someone and demand a ransom, then you might as well target the richest man in the world.

Mind you, it had not been easy. His planning, as always, was meticulous. Tracking down the grand daughter at that second rate school had proved difficult. He had searched all the 'rich' schools in the USA to no avail. Who'd have thought a billionaire would send his grand daughter to such a second rate school. But he didn't care now, he was moments away from his accomplice returning with the ransom in used notes and then HE would be on his way, alone.

This was his fourth kidnapping. He was getting better with each one. All had been a success, but never anywhere near this amount of money. He'd never been caught. He'd made sure there were no witnesses, including the kidnapped victim. He was getting good at this. He wondered sometimes whether he did it for the money or for the 'high' he got from such. The ultimate payback for those rich bastards. Steal their hard earned cash, put them through anguish during the kidnap phone calls and then make them suffer for ever more at the loss of their loved one. He, therefore, always made the 'killing' the most depraved his mind could conjure up and so heighten the delight in what some might say, his sordid mind.

He checked his suitcase, his passport, his wallet, his tickets, his handgun and silencer. He checked them all three times such was his paranoia. He went through a mental to-do list. Just a couple of problems to sort out, quietly, when his partner returned and then there would be no evidence at all. He had had some doubts about his partner but decided he was too dumb to try and double cross him.

It was getting late. Nothing could go wrong. It had all gone so well. The rich grandfather had even guaranteed anonymity as he did not want the police or the press involved. What a mug. His sense of privacy had gone against him and all he had to deal with now was his partner and that other small blind folded, problem in the back bedroom.

Suddenly all the lights went out. What now, he thought. He was always wary so he went to the window. The whole street had gone out. Typical he thought, but then again, only a little longer to wait for his money.

The four man HOE Team had cut the power to the whole street. They did not want the kidnapper to think it was only his house. Their leader was on a mission. He had let his Boss down all those years ago. Despite their best efforts he and his team had just got there too late on that one particular occasion. They were better now, a hell of a lot better. Years of practice!
He lived with that failed moment all his life, not that the Boss blamed him. He was that kind of guy. Since then they had sorted out a lot of things for the Boss. Though very well paid - it was done more so with a sense of duty. Each of his team and he absolutely believed in what

they were doing. Totally dissimilar to their past military and government experience where many a time they had questioned their orders. This time, they were 100% behind their Boss. Not only in their belief in him, but also at the job in hand. Well, they were not going to let the Boss down this time. So much so, that he was going to make sure that everything went well.

This one was personal. As said, many years ago he had let the family down. He wasn't going to do the same again.

The kidnapper decided to have a few minutes rest and lay on the couch. Maybe because his mind had been working at a million miles per hour he dozed off.

He half awoke as something disturbed him.

H.

THE BIOMEDICAL PROFESSOR

The Biomedical Professor could not believe it. He read the letter again and again and then looked at the enclosed cheque. Could it be true? Surely, these things only happen in books and films. He wondered how he could verify the cheque. There were a lot of scams going on in the modern world. He Googled the name on the cheque to make sure it wasn't a hoax. After all, it's not everyday you get a cheque for $80m.

Sure enough it was him. He thought back to their first meeting. It was a seminar somewhere in Denver. Although he hadn't met him during the day, moreso the evening in the hotel bar. At first he thought he was another Professor trying to find out exactly what he was up to. But he quickly thought otherwise. The benefactor seemed so interested in his work and his ideas. He quoted terms and hypotheses that only someone who was interested in his work would know. He could have understood this more so, if the guy was himself, suffering from prostate cancer, but he wasn't. He just genuinely wanted to know about his work and see if he could help in any way. He literally was a dream come true.

He had thought long and hard about the offer. After all some things are too good to be true. For a long time the young researcher was dismayed at his work and the effect of chemotherapy on cancer sufferers. He kept asking himself, 'Surely there was a better way than bombarding the body with X rays.'

His ultimate vision was to design a biomedical computer that could monitor a person's well being continually, then automatically deliver the right amount of drugs, blood, insulin to the appropriate areas etc etc to maintain and improve their health. Not to do away with staff but even the best nurses and doctors couldn't be there 24/7. His computer would supplement their work. Not replace them and enable them to do the other fine work that their job required.

His benefactor was extremely interested in this particular aspect of his work. He had tried to work out why. But then he decided, why waste time doing that, who cares? He'd been promised money before at various events were it turned out they were just trying to impress those gathered, But this chap had come up with the cash, a lot of cash, as he had promised. Anyone who is prepared to write a cheque for $80m - well basically, he did not care what his motives were. His invention could not be used unlawfully so why worry?

12.

THE CONTAINERS

Later the following day, once again the Detective was walking down the High Street when he saw MB (remember now a trillionaire in the Detective's eye) walking towards him. Typically no bodyguard. They both acknowledged each other and the Detective thought it was about time he bought the man a drink. Maybe not an expensive one, but hey it's the thought that counts. When he thought about it later, he thought, did he first came up with the idea of a drink or did MB prompt him. Either way he probably had more than he should have, definitely more than MB, but he put that down to his heavy heart in regard to his niece.

Either way, he suddenly found himself, sat beside the oligarch, in the back of his limo whisking him along an unknown motorway. Somehow, MB knew about his niece. How could that be? Had he spoken of her whilst slightly under the influence? He was talking about similar occurrences - where families had lost loved ones and been destined to sadness for the rest of their lives, whereas the perp simply got a few years of 'so called hard' labour. Was that fair? Where was the justice? What about the families? What about the anniversary of the death or rape, when the families were probably at their lowest ebb and yet ultimately the perp would be free as a bird and definitely not be thinking of his victim or victims. What about Christmases, Birthdays, Anniversaries were once again the perp would probably be celebrating elsewhere whilst the family had to handle all the grief. Where was the justice in that? What had the courts done to assist and help desperate families? Particularly in instances were the released perp went on to commit other horrendous crimes (as is often the case) and so create more bereaved families. Is that what society wanted? Is that what the public deserved? Wasn't there a better way? A way that would reduce recidivist crime! All of these words and statements were swimming around in the Detective's liquor fuelled mind.

After about one hour, but who knows, the Detective found them pulling up outside an old remote farmhouse in the middle of nowhere. There were no other farms or even buildings to be seen. He had tried to monitor the route but to no avail. They parked up at the front of the old farm house and his rich 'friend' invited him to accompany him around the back of the large, somewhat derelict building having left the chauffeur with the car. It was obviously an unused farm, for several years judging by the state of the buildings. The Detective's mind was racing. What was he doing here at an old rambling farmhouse with a trillionaire.

As they rounded the corner of the building a new blue, large steel container, caught the Detective's eye. The type you see on ships transporting items, but slightly out of place on an old farm. There was something else odd about it. He noticed, strangely, various electrical wires leading into the container that seemed out of place. On the outside they were wired up to a rather large generator. What was also strange that as opposed to everything else the container and the generator seemed brand new. The Detective's mind was in police mode, 'But why power up a storage container with so many wires? In a disused farm. At the most all it needed was a light and it looks as though these two items have just been placed here. No sign of weathering or dust'.

The trillionaire opened the container and various lights came on automatically. The Detective had a problem adjusting to the bright lights and he wasn't sure whether it was the alcohol, the stifled hot air or the ambience. As he refocused he saw a large well constructed, secure cage inside the container with small pipes and leads leading to what appeared to be a machine like you see at the side of a hospital bed. The lighting was not that good and he had difficulty focusing but once again he was unsure whether or not that may be the alcohol. The cage reminded him of something you would use to house a large cat during transportation. No one was going to break out of a cage like that. He slowly followed the pipes from the machine through the bars into the cage. But what was that? His mind froze. He had predicted every eventuality but not this. What the Hell. Whatever it was it made him reach for his firearm.

He blinked and did a double take. Was he hallucinating? Was he 'drunk?' But there, in the cage, lying on the bed, connected to the pipes was a human form, a body. His host could obviously see he was affected and he delicately touched his arm as if not to further alarm him. Just as he felt MB's touch the Detective realised that the body was not human; it was only a mannequin. He slumped down in a chair, once again not sure whether his current state was due to the alcohol, his shocked state, the extremely hot temperature in the container, the flashing lights or what he had just seen. Whilst he was dealing with this the trillionaire was talking.

He said, 'As opposed to having a simple (idyllic for him) life in prison, what if the perp was attached to such a machine. A machine that released a poison during his every waking moment. Not enough to kill him, mind, as that would be murder. But certainly enough poison to cause him pain and a pain equal to the barbaric crime he had committed. Added to that, what if the victim's families knew this was taking place. That each day they were suffering, they knew that the perp, the one responsible for their grief, their plight, was also suffering. The victims families knew their sadness would last to their dying day, but they also knew, so too would the perp suffer to his natural dying day. Doesn't that sound a far better system than what we have now. At the very least it would end recidivists walking the streets as free as a bird.' MB was looking at him intently.

The Detective's mind was awash but he was sobering. He was sobering up very quickly. He remembered, later, telling MB that this was preposterous, absurd, beyond belief, it couldn't work. He couldn't take, no one could take the law, or rather the sanctions into their own hands. It was kidnapping, assault, possibly manslaughter or at worst murder. He did, however, have the idea of pushing MB, before turning him down flat. He wanted to know how he would acquire victims or perps as if he was going along with it. When questioned as to how he would go about 'obtaining' the perp MB answered thus.

'Such 'inmates' would be 'acquired' in a variety of ways. From the prison steps on their release, or captured having escaped from prison or possibly, during the course of their crime before any police involvement. Either way they would always be 100% guilty, no room for doubt. Any examples less than 100% guilty would be left to the authorities as is.'

Later, before the limo dropped him off, MB assured him that, of course, 'No crime has taken place. It was a mannequin. There was no real poison. It was a mere enactment of my thoughts as to why society was failing victims. No crime had been committed. No harm done. It was the whim of rich people, Michael Jackson had his monkeys, Richard Branson wants to fly to Mars, we even have a multi millionaire in the White House'.

The Detective was dropped off at home and soon fell into a very, alcohol induced deep sleep. Dreaming of drugged up murdering mannequins, terrorising the neighbourhood and hiding in storage containers that flew like giant zeppelins across the landscape.

I.

THE TERRORIST

The driver drove his van very carefully. So would you if you knew what he had on board. He made sure his team had chosen a route without speed ramps. Everything was going so well. They had planned this attack for months. The van was actually an ice cream van making its way to a summer fayre in the city centre. It was estimated there would be in excess of 100,000 at the fayre, mainly women and children. 'Who on earth would stop an ice cream van,' his team had thought.

The terrorists had thought about everything. Too many mistakes had been made in the past. They did dummy run after dummy run to make sure of their route. An ordinary ice cream van. However in place of ice cream and the necessary paraphernalia to make such was a 1700 kg bomb set to a remote controlled timer. All he had to do was park it in an allotted place right beside all the crowds, put a sign in the window stating GONE TO LUNCH and then get as far away as quickly as possible before detonating the bomb by remote control on his phone.

He was making good time. Traffic was light. He was going to be on time. But then the traffic slowed down right in front of him. He could see the cause, 2 cars ahead. It appeared that two light vans had either collided or broken down. The one behind had the bonnet open and the driver noticed that the two van drivers were female. Not only female but young, very good looking, long legs right up to there very short, and skimpy shorts. They both seemed in a quandary and they were holding him up. He probably would have assisted them no matter what they looked like as he needed to get past but the fact that they're looked as they did probably clouded his mind a little.

He made sure that his ice cream van was close enough to the two vans not to be interfered with. He then vacated his van, locked it and made his way to the van with the 'open bonnet' and the two girls. One of them was leaning over the bonnet; everything was on display. He came up behind her, enjoying the view, and asked them if he could help.

In a very Southern accent, the one leaning over the bonnet turned slightly and said, 'Oh my dear Lord. Look, a knight in shining armour. Oh please, I don't know a battery from a carburetor. It just died on me. Could you take a look please? My girlfriend is just getting a pair of jump leads from the back of her truck just in case.'

Out of the corner of his eye he noticed the other driver raising the shutters on the back of her van. The southern lass went on, 'I'd or rather we'd be ever so grateful if you could help, if you know what I mean,' and she curtsied and bit her bottom lip. He almost fell over himself to assist and leant over the bonnet next to her. Her legs were just as good as her bosom which was on open display as she leant over the bonnet. He was concentrating on them far more than he was concentrating on the engine.

That's probably why he didn't notice the other driver approach him from behind, syringe in hand. He thought she was cuddling up to him from behind when suddenly he felt a sharp prick in his neck. Instantly he felt faint, his legs gave way and he blanked out.

As he did so one of the girls caught his shoulders, the other lifted his feet and they quickly scooped him up into the back of the open truck were their two ex SAS colleagues were waiting. They quickly searched him and took his keys and his mobile phone.

One of the male HOE Team jumped out of the van and shut the shutters. Both female drivers got into their vans. The male operative with the keys and the phone made his way to the ice cream van. The convoy of three vehicles were then escorted from the scene by two 'look alike' police cars on blues and twos driven by another two colleagues.

The HOE Team now numbered five. They wended their way through as many quiet streets as possible until they reached their destination. Once inside the disused warehouse the 'bomber's lifeless body was moved to another vehicle. A seventh member of the team, who had spent all his army life disarming bombs, approached the ice cream van. It was a rudimentary bomb and easily disarmed within 3 minutes. The fact that they had been monitoring the terrorist team for months certainly helped.

All the team members then got on the vehicle with the 'bomber' and then made their way to a second destination well outside the city. As they made their way the bomber was coming around.

As he did he noticed that his hands and feet were secured. He could not move. The seats were in a conference style and one of the team was facing the bomber.

The young female commander, now without the Southern drawl said, "We reckon that your 'ice cream van' as it were could possibly have killed anywhere between 5-10 thousand people and that's a conservative guess. However, this time it's not going to cause anything, it won't even get a parking ticket. Not like your last little escapade in London. I think the death toll there was 222 wasn't it.

Well we have a benefactor, as it were, who has decided that the world would be far better off if you weren't running around doing whatever you and your cronies want to do. There are several families in London who think the same thing. Your two colleagues as well, we have just picked them up. So we are going to take you to somewhere where you cannot cause anyone, anymore grief.'

As the ex soldier turned away she added, 'For the rest of your Goddamn miserable life.'

13.

MORE BAD NEWS

Over the next few days the Detective constantly thought about what had gone on. Maybe the guy was actually crazy after all? Is that what happens when you've got so much money you don't know what to do with it? He thought back to the programme he had seen. "Who wants to be a billionaire?" None of them were normal. In his mind's eye, they had risen above, or below, their fellow man and woman. They no longer looked the same, acted the same, spoke the same. Rich enough to live out their fantasies no matter how far fetched they were. Abramovich with his submarine like yacht. Branson with his space ships. Boys and their toys he thought. So MB may have been crazy but he had also been right in his summation. At the end of the day, no crime had been committed.

Exactly one week later the Detective got a call out of the blue to his mother's house at 2am. He knew that if she was calling at that time it must be serious. She was unable to explain herself over the phone hence his attendance in the middle of the night.

As he approached the house on a very cold, winter evening his heart feared the worst. His mother had never been seriously ill. Approaching his retirement he feared the irony of losing his mother after already losing his wife and son. To his surprise, at the kitchen table was his mother and her sister, his aunt. They were crying. His niece had passed away at midnight. Both women were inconsolable. The Detective went and got a $6.5k bottle of wine from the boot of his car. Throughout the following few hours they got through another 2 bottles from the car. It broke his heart to see the two people he loved most in the world, grieving so. Despite everything, if he could have got his hands around the throat of the pimp, who ultimately murdered his niece and brought about this heartache, he would have squeezed the living daylights out of him.

If he thought that was bad, about one month later, his aunt took her own life. Unable to face life without her daughter, unable to face what she thought she should have done or could have done to prevent such. Again, he found himself drinking late into the night with his mother. He was now all she had left. He remembered some so-called advise he had been given from a Commander years ago. He had been sideswiped by the news that a 32 year old colleague had suddenly died from a brain hemorrhage. Not two months beforehand they had just successfully completed a charity event climbing three tall mountains. On top of that it was the third 30 plus colleague he had lost in a year to natural (if you can call them that) causes. When the Commander walked in and saw him bereft he expected some consoling words of advise. However, what he was told was to 'man up', get used to the fact that as you got older then everyone you know gets older and that basically this was to become a regular event. More funerals than weddings. Turns out the bastard was right. Every few months he learnt of another death of someone he knew.

The 'perp', who had never been prosecuted, had claimed two lives as far as he was concerned. Half drunk, he explained to his mother what the millionaire had suggested; he agreed such was due recompense for the 'pimp'. Strangling was too quick. The perp needed to suffer just like his niece, his aunt, his mother and himself were suffering. He wasn't too astounded when his mother looked him in the eye and said that that was far more justice than offered in any court. At 4am that morning, with his mother unable to sleep due to the heartache, in a drunken haze, at the lowest ebb of his life, he texted the millionaire with the following two words, 'Do it'.

14.

DRUNK TEXTS ARE NEVER A GOOD IDEA

The next morning or rather very early afternoon, the Detective awoke with a start. It took him a while to come to his senses as we all know what it's like when you have a 'good' evening. Gradually drunken images appeared in his head as he tried to fathom what had happened last night. It took him a few minutes as unbeknownst to most of the public a good night's sleep does not get rid of 'all' the alcohol. There are mores road deaths at 0600 than 1800 due to people who think they have 'slept off' the night before.

He came to a start and suddenly remembered what he had done. At first he could not believe he had done something so rash. It went against everything he stood for regarding law and order. He kept telling himself it was a dream. The he looked at his phone. All those cliches about not texting messages when you were drunk came rushing at him.

He quickly dialled the millionaire. Such was his condition that at first he dialled a totally random number and started to implore them to disregard his text. It took awhile for the befuddled receiver to explain it was a wrong number. This time the Detective was careful. He desperately hoped he would answer. After four rings MB answered.

'Errr, I don't quite know how to say this and please forgive me for disturbing you. But my mother and I received some bad news, well some further bad news last night and I had a little more than I am used to, drink wise. I don't know if you know what that's like but some people do strange things after a good drink. Hence my text which of course I want to retract as it was made after a heavy drinking session.'

MB calmly replied, 'Of course, I understand Detective. Grief like yours can cause such and I do offer my most sincere condolences to you and your mother in regard to your aunt. But don't worry. Don't worry at all. Absolutely nothing will happen as a result of your phone call or rather text.'

The Detective put the phone down thankful that he had just stopped becoming a conspirator to several crimes. He vowed to A) treat that expensive wine with a lot more respect, B) Not text when drunk, ever, and C) be very careful of any future conversation with MB.

He did however think about MB's words. Hell, he always thought about MBs words as here was a man who did not get where he was by either saying the wrong thing or even implying such. 'Nothing will happen as a result of your phone call or rather text.' He pondered on such for a few minutes. No, no misinterpretation could be made. MB had stated categorically that he would not do anything as a result of his text. Back at home, he sat down or rather slumped down. As he drifted off he again had a bad dream that he had not woken up in time and his cousin's perp was being abducted. He later woke up with a start. Checked the time. Checked his phone. No, it was just a bad dream.

The weeks and months passed as he 'marched' or on occasion 'plodded' his way towards his retirement. He was once again beginning to enjoy himself; planning, drawing up lists, window shopping. He felt as if he was the happiest he had been for quite some time. He was about to take a new lease of life at quite a young age. Most people never get that opportunity. They slog their guts out until 65 or even older in today's modern world and then are too knackered to enjoy their retirement as they would wish. He was going to make the most of it.

He could even endure his two supervisors. It was if they were determined to make his last few months as difficult as possible. But the harder they tried the more he did not let them get to him. Despite their ranks, he was the better man. Not in his own mind's eye. But his 'troops' could see what was going on and they rallied around him. He thought, 'You don't get that because of your rank. You earn that no matter what your rank. He was convinced that most police forces in the world ran on the two lowest ranks. If all the other ranks got sacked the police would still go on. If the two lowest ranks got sacked then the law and order would grind to a halt. He thought of a saying he had never forgotten and it probably summed up all police forces. They were Lions supervised by monkeys.

He often thought about 'howlers' from senior officers he had experienced. A Commander who wanted to put windows in an office to save on air conditioning charges only to be informed that the office was 4 floors underground! Another wanted to save money by getting rid of all the sections houses that were used to house new recruits. He was politely informed that there was a recruitment drive on as police numbers had dwindled and they desperately needed more accommodation, not less. And finally, when he was a young sergeant, a senior office asked him to organise school crossing patrols during the school holidays! You couldn't really make it up. He honestly believed that you more your rise to the top the more you get cut off from everyday life. Maybe they had done him a great favour by not letting him rise through the ranks. He and the officers around him, were a lot better of for such.

However Life is never easy it it? Where is the only place you can go to when you are at the top? What always happens when you are deliriously happy and content? Tragedy strikes. Doom and gloom!

J.

THE DOCTOR

The Doctor was particularly looking forward to today. Not everyday you meet your rich benefactor without whom none of this would be possible. His dream had come true. At times he had to pinch himself to make sure it wasn't all a dream.

He had set up a research hospital in Florida to deal with the increase in deaths due to Tarantula spiders and other venomous reptiles. Rather than see the spider as a predator, he believed there were other benefits to the poison carried by the female spider. She could be a lifesaver and not a partner killer.

All he needed was the money to further his research. The trouble was no one believed him. Not until this man; and that was were the man he was about to meet came into the picture. Out of the blue, he had contacted the Doctor, asked him about his work and then come up with a cheque for $40m, which was more than he needed.

He was looking forward to showing this 'Saint' around the research laboratories where he had done several experiments on the Tarantulas poison. He had made quite a few amazing, startling discoveries.

He couldn't wait to show off his achievements.

The richest man on the planet was getting out of his helicopter and approaching the Doctor. He couldn't wait to hear what this young man had to say about all the poisons he was researching. This was the final part of his plan. The $40m was money very well spent.

15.

THE FUNERAL

More than anything the Detective wanted to retire and treat his mother to things both she and he had never been able to afford. She had had a hard life. Luxuries were a mystery to her. Her life had been one hard slog. He was going to reward her in his retirement. The money would not be just for him. He was going to treat her like a Queen. He had never told her. He wanted it to be a surprise. How much he regretted that now. He was so close. They were so close.

At his mother's funeral he thought about her, obviously. Undoubtedly, the loss of her sister and niece had weighed heavily on her mind and heart, possibly costing her a few months, if not years. He felt very sad, bitter even. He had kept himself very much to himself desperately trying to deal with his loss. Police officers deal with death all the time, it's part of the job. You think you get used to it, hardened. But when it was your own kin, well that's a totally different story.

At the funeral whilst his mind wandered, again, something, someone, made him remember his sixth sense. It took awhile but finally she caught his eye. It was a youngish woman. He had never seen her before and he knew she wasn't family. But she looked very familiar.
He was thinking about this later, at the wake, when he came across a distant cousin. He asked her about the young woman he had seen

earlier. His cousin said that she wasn't too sure who she was. She had seen her a few times when she came round to see his mother, the young woman had been having tea with her. All this seemed strange to the Detective. Why had his mother not mentioned such? Why did she look familiar? The problem with a police officer is that you come across so many people. Sometimes, you can't even remember which side of the fence they came from. He remembered once an Inspector button holing him, trying to recall how he knew him. Well the Detective did know him. He'd interviewed him over a horrendous complaint which didn't go anywhere but it scotched the Inspectors chance of promotion in the future. He prayed the Inspector did not remember him. Which brought him back. Who was she!

As his cousin walked away, she remembered the woman's surname. When she told the Detective, he dropped his glass of wine. People stared. It was the same surname as MB. He grabbed hold of his cousin, so hard that people looked at him. He asked her, demanded of her, that she explain exactly what she had seen, what she had heard, everything. His cousin was somewhat startled but could obviously see that this was important to him. She related again the same memory of the young woman, in the kitchen, sat down, drinking tea, talking to his mother.

She halted for a few seconds and then she remembered that there was something else that was strange. There were some official looking papers on the table and her mother was signing them. The Detective froze. His mind raced backwards. Despite him cancelling the millionaire, had he gone behind his back and convinced his mother to go ahead with his crazy plan? His mind went into overload in regard to what he should or could do. This was the day of his mother's funeral, for God's sake. Then, the Detective's analytical police mind kicked in.

He rushed out to his car, started the engine and roared around to the millionaire's mansion.

16.

THE MANSION

He screeched to a halt outside the mansion and ran up to the large front door, banging on it with both fists. What only can be described as a butler opened the door and before he could utter a word the Detective burst past him. He knew where the millionaire normally spent his day in his office/library. He made his way there and swung the door open. It was obvious the millionaire was sat in a large leather chair, with his back to him facing a bank of TV monitors. He noticed that they all turned off as he entered.

He immediately launched into a extremely loud tirade, accusing the millionaire of going behind his back, manipulating a frail, old woman, deliberately cutting him out because he knew the Detective would never agree to such. The Detective was virtually spitting as he heaped accusation upon accusation upon the millionaire.

The chair slowly turned around. Sat in the chair was the young woman from the funeral, the spitting image of MB. At this point the Detective noticed the Butler and two very large and armed, security men entering the office at speed. The young woman looked at the Detective and then informed her staff, in an authoritative tone, that the police officer was not going to be a problem. They were going to have a civil conversation and she asked them to leave. As she said this she looked, intently, at the Detective. She then invited him to sit down.

'She was definitely related to MB,' thought the Detective.

She then said in a very soft, controlled and calming voice, 'Detective, I presume you are the police officer of whom my father spoke of many, many times and, may I say, always favourably. That is why I am going to ignore your spurious accusations and talk calmly to you. Out of respect to my father. But I would ask firstly, that you do not raise your voice and have due reverence to my father who died in his sleep, very peacefully, four months ago'.

The Detective sat down, open mouthed. He did not know he was dead, he definitely did not know he had a daughter and he was having problems, at this point in time, of putting any jigsaws together.

She went on, 'Firstly Detective, may I offer my condolences to you and your family. Having recently lost my father I understand what it is like to lose a parent. Maybe today is not a good day to have this conversation, but I feel that you want and need answers. But let me say this. I do not have to tell you anything. But since my father spoke so highly of you I feel that I can explain some things to you. Of course, there is no such thing as off the record but if you attempt to use anything that I say against me, I will, of course, deny everything.'

'The fact of the matter is that neither my father nor I approached your mother. He acted on your instructions to cancel any actions after the awful death of your niece and aunt. He respected your instructions. However, in actual fact your mother approached us and if there is any doubt over this in your mind's eye I can prove everything I say via recordings and various documentation. She informed us exactly what she wanted. Part of her request was that you should not know anything about this. She was of the definite opinion that you would try and stop her. I can tell you that she was very, very happy with our arrangement. Part of the reason I was at her funeral was that she said both my father and myself were the only people who had helped her and made her feel better since the death of her sister and niece.'

The Detective's mouth was agape; he was truly astounded. A very unusual feeling in the Detective's world. So much information, so little time to compute and all very personal. Had his mother really distrusted him that much? Had this young woman and her father brought solace to her in her final days? Was he really that far adrift of what his mother wanted, what she needed?

But then the Detective part of his brain cut in. This was a crime, a conspiracy, a felony. He started hurling further accusations, at which point the young woman stated she had nothing else to say and invited him to leave in a way that implied if he didn't leave voluntarily, then he would be ejected. He chose the voluntary route.

But as he left, she said, 'Remember Detective, your mother's involvement in all of this. Mud sticks. I trust you understand?'

K.

THE CHILD MURDERER

Inside a sealed container the 'child kidnapper, rapist, butcher, murderer' lay on the steel bed, restricted by the bonds around his feet and hands. His head held in static position by more restraints. He knew what was going to happen. The thought was almost as horrific as the act. He pretended to be asleep. It was the only time he got any peace. What really got to him was, 'Why was he here?' It was undoubtedly some sort of payback. But for which one of his many crimes? The fact was that he had committed so many horrific crimes that he couldn't think which one caused all this.

Maybe, he thought of the 9 year old he had snatched, butchered and killed and not been caught. Then there was the 12 year old he had kidnapped, raped and killed and once again evaded capture. Or even the 13 year old he had enticed into his van, tortured, raped and then disposed of the body in a wood chipper. And those were just the ones he remembered. There were many, many more. But he had no remorse for any of these, remembered or forgotten. He just wanted to know which crime had earned him this.

His mind was reeling. How long would he be here? Was there an end to it? He had no idea? Maybe if he knew about the cage next to him that he could just about see, It was set up exactly like his but in this cage the tubes were connected to a skeleton. The mere sight of it made it even more horrific.

The he heard it. Always at exactly the same time of day, like clockwork. The electrical buzz, the 'hiss' of a piston, electric circuits transmitting their commands. The machine was starting up. He knew what was going to happen. There wasn't a thing he could do. He didn't even try to resist anymore, it was futile.

As the poison ventured it's way along the tubes it finally entered his body. He let out a blood curdling scream. It was as though 10,000 volts had been passed through his entire body. As though he was being bitten by a million mosquitos. He writhed against the straps. They allowed a little movement, for reasons explained later.

A pain far more so than any of his victims suffered as in this case he knew this was not the end. Unlike his victims who had an end to absolute pain and misery upon their death. But not for him. No escape like his victims. His would never end, like his victim's families. His happened very day. His body was wracked in pain, it was a blood curdling scream to end all screams. A scream that could be heard by no one so it certainly wasn't for effect. This was true, unadulterated, searing pain. A pain he had no control over. A pain he could not stop. A pain he did not feel he deserved. An enduring horrendous pain that no human could ever forget much the same as his victims families.

Although one small fact that never entered his tiny little sordid mind, it was a pain possibly akin to what his victims endured during his crimes. The only consolation for the innocent was that their pain was mostly quick and they knew it was the end. A terrifying thought in itself but what if you knew that you were going to experience that pain every day for the rest of your life. Would you say a 'just' penalty. You can bet your last dollar that the mothers and fathers of the 9, 12 and 13 year old thought it justified!

Attached to a wall behind him a video camera automatically zoomed in on his face and recorded every single second in glorious Hi Definition technicolor.

17.

BACK AT THE OFFICE

The Detective went back to his office, his mind reeling. He knew he was absolutely sober as he had not drunk anything at the funeral. No, this time his mind was fuelled by something. Was it revenge? Was it his police officer's mind? This was the day of his his mother's funeral but he had just received information that could implicate her in a major crime.

The only person present back at his office was the young detective. In desperation the Detective poured his heart out and told him everything. Every last detail. As a result they pondered on what they could do. Could it be true? How could they investigate this matter? They checked on the PNC the name of his niece's pimp; NO TRACE; he seemed to have vanished off the face of the earth!

It then hit the Detective like a bulldozer. Could there be others? They decided to check on the status of 'perps' released within the last six months. On average 20% would go missing naturally for a variety of reasons; vendettas, new life elsewhere, new identity, natural and unnatural death. However their PNC showed that 68% seemed to be 'missing'. The Detective put his head in his hands. Could this crazy old millionaire have actually carried out his 'mission? How was it possible although it reminded him that if you had enough money maybe you could achieve anything? No matter how far from the norm. It might explain the alarming rise in figures. But how could they trace 'perps' that had gone missing?

For 48 hours the Detective racked his brain. He didn't care if it meant taking down the young woman or anyone else for that matter. This was too big. It just wasn't right. No one could take this on outside the courts. It went against his whole raison d'etre as a police officer, everything he had been preaching for 29 years.

One morning the young detective burst into his office. He was breathless. He regaled a story of a young rich kid that had gone off the rails several years ago. He had been involved in a bungled shop raid where the shopkeeper, his wife and two assistants had been fatally wounded. After serving 12 years he had been released on probation but was now one of the 68% that had gone missing.

The Detective did not see how this could help until he was told that the rich kid's father had had him 'chipped' when he was 6 years old after there had been a spate of kidnappings in their area. It would appear that there was a chance the chip had never been removed and if so they might be able to trace him.

They immediately started researching and phoning 'chipping' companies. There were 100's if not 1000's of them.

They had almost lost hope when finally a possible trace came up. It turned out the chip was indeed an old one. They then learnt that therefore any trace would need to be close to the source, the tracer. Not easy but, yes, it was still up and working!

18.

THE FLIGHT

That is why, three days later the Detective sat in a waiting room at JFK airport, with a Techy, from the 'chipping' company who was feverishly typing away on a laptop. There was also an ex Vietnam pilot who was explaining about the helicopter that they were all about to be transported within. Finally there was an FBI agent.

The Detective had decided to go above his two supervisors. He knew they would scupper his case no matter how big it was. He had a few favours to be called in on the run up to his retirement and this was one of them. He had done enough favours for a few Commanders that he knew exactly which one to go to to get his job sanctioned. He had secured all the paperwork and necessary documents to completely overrule anything his immediate supervisors might have come up with to stop him.

However once the Detective had explained everything to the Commander and the fact he was more than aware that they may need to cross boundaries, the senior officer had insisted that he involve the FBI. That is why he had quite a few meetings with them explaining his case. He half expected them to bail out and say there was nothing in it but the Detective had almost 30 years experience and he knew how to present a case. Hence, today.

The Techy was responsible for working the laptop and associated equipment that could follow the signal from the 'chip'. The pilot was chosen for his past 'war' experience and his undoubted ability piloting a helicopter. The FBI agent had been fully briefed by his commanding officers.

As explained previously, because the 'chip' was so old, they had not immediately locked onto it. Later 'chips' were more powerful but this one was pre 1995 so it had a limited range. It had taken some time covering vast areas of the USA until finally they had identified that it was now within 100 miles of the airport; hence their gathering.

The Detective was 'psyched'. He knew that on the one hand they may find nothing, But on the other, they could find the rich 'perp' and gain enough evidence to mount a substantial case. He wanted to reward his young protege for all his work but there were only 4 seats in the helicopter. The pilot had been given limited information, the techy only knew they needed to find a chip, the FBI agent knew everything and more.

They boarded the helicopter at midday and took off. There was a slight delay as the FBI agent had to take an urgent telephone call, or that's what he called it, before they took off.

Immediately they were aloft the techy started to direct the pilot according to his box of tricks. All the Detective could hear, apart from the helicopter, was the faint bleep from the Techys equipment. This went on for some time. Some loud 'beeps', some quiet 'bleeps'. As said, the Detective was 'wired'.

Suddenly, the bleeps got louder and louder but the helicopter was heading out towards the Atlantic. The Detective's mind was running at a million miles an hour. Had the container been dumped in the sea to evade capture? Had the body been dumped in the sea? Had the chip been removed and thrown overboard? The bleeps got louder and louder as they rounded the coast

As the Detective looked around the headland he suddenly realised why. Everything now made sense.

19.

THE BLEEPS

The bleeps were now, in the Detective's head, as loud as the roar of the helicopter's engines and rotors. Up ahead was a huge container ship, as big as an oil tanker and on its deck were hundreds of steel storage containers.

All the Detective could think was, 'Oh my God!' What had he (MB) done? He was so busy trying to conjure such up in his mind, he did not see or hear the FBI agent relaying the ships details to someone over his radio.

He also didn't hear the pilot stating that his helicopter was equipped with a heat detector system to detect body heat. Although he could get faint traces in the containers there were apparently no crew at all on the tanker. The pilot went on to say that he had come across these ghost ships in Vietnam totally run by a computer with no staff on board. He then went on to say that they kept well away from these Ghost ships. If the enemy were that protective that they would not put any staff aboard, then how well armed were they? From his experience they were always very well armed.

At this point the FBI ended his radio call abruptly and then immediately ordered the pilot to abort the mission and return whence they came.

He tried to explain why to the Detective, but all the Detective was thinking, and acknowledging, was that the evidence was on board that ship and that's why they were going to land on it.

He later reasoned with himself as to why, at that point he drew his firearm, pointed it at the FBI agent and told the pilot to land on the ship. The FBI agent was shouting, the pilot was shouting, the Detective was pointing his side arm at everyone, bar the Techy, and shouting. The helicopter slowly approached the tanker.

That's when it happened. A sudden explosion that catapulted the helicopter out of control. Helicopter alarms went off, lights flashed and the pilot fought with the controls as a blinding fireball emanated from the ship. The occupants were thrown about in the helicopter and the Detective lost his firearm. What the hell had happened?

20.

THE AFTERMATH

Two hours later the Detective was sat, forlornly in an office at JFK Airport, alone. He was thinking about the last few hours. What else was there to think about? The ship was totally and utterly destroyed. It transpired that they thought it had a self arming destruction system which was activated if anything got too close. The Detective then remembered the Pilot's words re Ghost ships. Apparently there wasn't a part of it left, bigger than your fist. The explosion was immense. What ever was aboard, including the ship itself, was now at the bottom of a very deep ocean and totally irretrievable. Even if they could get, to it, it would be worthless as the pressure at the bottom of ocean floor at 8000 feet would have destroyed everything.

Ultimately it would appear, the FBI agent, on reflection, had sympathised with the Detective and altered his evidence so apparently 'no firearm' was drawn. The Pilot and Techy went along with such, they were just happy to be alive.

The Detective smiled to himself. He should have known. If there had been a perp in every container then the deceased trillionaire would have made sure no evidence could ever be gleaned or come back to him or his daughter. It was later estimated that there were 250 containers on the deck and also, that such a ship could have 500 containers below the deck.

He never did find out why the FBI agent tried to cancel the mission. He didn't care anymore. To tell the truth he'd had enough. He had other priorities. In the last few months he'd lost his mother, his aunt, his niece. It had been the final straw that broke the camel's back. If it had to be something telling him it was the end, it might as well be this.

Maybe a part of him agreed with the Trillionaire. Even if only what had been achieved for his mother. If he, if they, had made her happy in her final days, then maybe that was justice. Maybe far more justice than she would have got anywhere else. He asked himself one question. It was the question he asked himself everytime he had made a major decision and it had borne him well through the years, even though it has not been mentioned until now. The question was quite simply, 'If I could ask 7 billion people about my decision, would the majority agree?' He reckoned they would agree, unanimously, with the trillionaire. He smiled to himself. He looked upwards. His wife and son, is two colleagues, his aunt, his niece and his mother were all smiling at him and giving him the thumbs up.

All he wanted to do now was to retire. To hell with it all. Little did he know about his 'Saints' that would look after him for the rest of his life.

21.

THE MULTI BILLIONAIRESS

The trillionairess sat at her desk, calmly. Her private phone rang. She knew who was calling. She let it ring five times and then answered it. As stated she knew the caller but more importantly the caller knew her. The caller informed and assured her that the loss of her ship and it's contents would be fully recompensed. The caller also hoped it would not affect or jeopardise any future business. He went on to say that the Detective would be dealt with as he had by far exceeded his jurisdiction. He had personally tried to intervene and cancelled the mission via an FBI agent on board the helicopter, but to no avail. The young lady listened, patiently and respectfully until the caller had finished. She knew and and more importantly he knew, she would have the last word. But she listened, her father had taught her well that it was always more important to listen than it was to talk.

Eventually she thanked him politely and reverently for the offer of compensation. However she declined such. She never wanted to be beholden to this person. He would never have the upper hand. Also she knew that he did not want to effect any future business, as between them they had reduced the USA's recidivist crime rate by 67%. Let alone the cost of housing all the perps.

But the question regarding the Detective. She remembered how fondly her father had talked about him. In many ways he lived a life that the trillionaire would have liked to live and therefore she wanted him to have a happy and long retirement. She made a point of telling the caller this. She did not want the Detective to have an unfortunate accident and from that point of view she would appoint a 'saint' to watch over him (she did not trust the caller and never would).

The caller thought back to his predecessor telling him about the young woman's father. He had been told, in no uncertain terms, that despite his office, this person was more powerful than he and he should not be crossed. He remembered his predecessor made a point of telling him this more than once. He was of the opinion that the young woman was exactly like her father and he had no intention of double crossing her. He thanked her and she ended by thanking him. 'Thank you Mr President' she said and then she hung up. As the President put the phone down, he shivered as if someone had walked over his grave.

The trillionairess leant back in her chair and switched on the 240 monitors on the huge wall in front of her. The vast majority showed an unsupervised container ship sailing the seas with anywhere between 200-600 containers aboard. They covered all 4 corners of the globe. The USA was not her only customer nor the only one to realise the benefits of what she had to offer.

22.

THE MONITORS

She then looked at Monitor 1. It showed a cage, within a container and in the cage was a skeleton. The lights were dimmed but you still make out the contents of the cage. He had died of natural causes many, many years ago. But she and her father had kept it. A memento as it were. She liked looking at the skeleton of the man that had kidnapped, raped and killed her mother all those years ago. Her poor father, upon learning of the kidnap had employed a crack Seal and SAS team to hunt down the kidnapper/s.

Although they had found him it was tragically too late to save his wife, her mother. Two other bodies were found in the kidnapper's lair. Via detection and DNA testing they traced the families and her father subsequently spoke to them.

He told them they had caught the kidnapper. They could hand him over to police but with a fancy lawyer, even if he was found guilty, he could be out in 15 years. He then put Plan B to them. What if they could arrange for him to suffer, just as they had to. What if they could make him suffer for as long as they had had to suffer, in other words, all theirs and his life. What if the suffering could be equal to theirs. Not housed in a fancy cell with access to a wide screen TV, radio, a gym, human company. Her father once told her that it took the families 30 seconds to decide on Plan B. Was this where her father formulated a plan and put such into action. A plan that would ultimately do more to reduce recidivist crime than any court, in any land, could ever do.

On monitor 2 was her daughter's kidnapper, alive and kicking, as they say, but that was probably due to the poison cursing through his veins. Her father could not believe it when the same thing had happened to his granddaughter. Once again he sent in his HOE Team but this time they saved the young girl, they caught the kidnapper (but not his sidekick as the Police got to him first). Her daughter was now housed in a private finishing school in Switzerland where no one knew who she was. They had both decided that was the best thing to do. Despite his trying to stay low key, even as a billionaire, he had had two loved ones kidnapped. He, or rather they, were not going to let it happen again. Maybe she was over cautious. But another HOE Team had been employed to watch her daughter from afar, 24/7.

She sighed. All the pain, all the hurt she had ever felt at the loss of her mother, at the kidnapping of her daughter was eased by the fact that none of those incarcerated could cause anyone, any more pain, ever again.

23.

THE HOE EMPLOYEE

The richest woman on the face of the earth's well dressed employee parked his company car outside the large and very neat house. He's been doing this job for six years. He liked it. Hell, he loved it.. He had met a lot of sad, disturbed, worried, nightmare ridden customers. But, as always he was welcomed into their homes. He, backed by his Company, bought them something no one else could. He brought them solace in a world of torture and torment.

The occupants of the house knew he was coming. This date was in their diary, permanently. It was a day burnt into their memory forever. Their darkest day of the year and they had a few others. Birthdays, Christmases, etc etc. However, today was the fourth anniversary of their dear daughter's tragic murder.

She had been grabbed from the street at 12 years old. The police report was not for the faint hearted. She had been repeatedly raped, tortured, sodomised and then eventually mutilated. Her body, or what was left of it, had never been found.

Her parents watched the employee set out his laptop on their kitchen counter, gently. He had them sign a few obligatory forms, said a few words and gave a few instructions. He then turned the laptop on but before doing so he advised them to sit down.

The screen on the laptop gradually grew to show a cage, within which was their daughter's assailant chained to a bed. He appeared to be asleep. Suddenly a machine, just outside the cage, burst into life, lit up and started to make a noise. They could see clear pipes leading from the machine into the cage. They could see different colour fluids making their way from the machine and along the pipes into the cage.

The screen suddenly cut to the assailant's face. He was most definitely awake now and also watching the pipes, intnely. He had a look of sheer terror on his face. He knew what was going to happen. As the poisons entered his body he let out an ear piercing, shrieking and his body racked backwards and forwards in absolute pain. The employee had long ago learnt to have his finger on the volume button at this stage. He allowed them to hear a little screaming, but would then turn the volume down so it did not become too distressing (if ever it could). Just enough for them to get the picture and feel very, very satisfied.

The husband then led his wife from the kitchen, sobbing, but vindicated, as the employee put away his equipment.

24.

THE MOTHER

Not wanting to disturb the grieving parents the employee then let himself out of the front door quietly and walked down the drive towards his unmarked and ordinary car. He felt as if he had done this a thousand times before. But then he heard someone behind him and turned around. As he did so he covered the firearm in his belt. One always had to be careful in his line of work. However, it was the mother. She was trotting in order to catch up with him. She was mist-eyed and teaul, but the crying had stopped. He stopped and faced her looking as reverent as possible. He kept a comfortable but respectful distance from her.

She said very softly, 'Please, I am sorry to delay you, but I wanted to say this.'

She took a few seconds and took a tissue from her trouser pocket. She took a deep breath. Her voice faltered as she spoke. She was quite obviously very emotional. The employee could not hear her properly so respectfully requested that she speak a little louder and repeat what she had said.

She took no offence at the request and repeated herself a little louder.

'Sorry, I know there are a lot of people who would not understand or agree with what we have just witnessed. I don't expect anyone to understand. I don't need them to understand. I don't blame them for that in actual fact I am glad that they don't have to understand., glad that they have not been put through the sheer hell and torture that we've been put through. I would never wish that on any living soul, any parent, any mother. But, the very sad fact is that the only thing that keeps me going these days is knowing that….that animal….that beast, that we have just seen, is suffering aswell.It is heartening to know that the pain my daughter must have gone through and the pain that we are going through, is as far as possible equally matched by the pain he is now suffering.'

She continued and with each word she was becoming more assured of herself..

'Please, please tell your employer that if ever they have cause to doubt themselves, if ever the liberal do-gooders get to them, to think on these words. I am sure there are parents in similar positions who would say the same. Your employer is the only person on the face of this planet who has shown us any compassion or true justice in out loss. No court, no judicial system, no judge, no prison, no welfare counsellors have come close. What you are doing allows myself and my husband to sleep a little better at night and even, at my lowest moments, at Christmases, at Birthdays, I can now think on what I have just witnessed. Horrific though it is, it brings us a degree of peace from out constant heartache. Please thank them from the bottom of our hearts.

The employee thanked her and promised he would pass on her words. As he did so, she turned around and walked back to her home. Her husband was waiting at the front door and as she approached him he put his arms around her. They stayed like that for quite some time.

What the employee would never have told her or the countless others that had thanked him and his company in a similar fashion, was that this was a very common scenario. Extremely grateful mothers, fathers, husbands, wives, brothers, sisters, teachers, loved ones etc etc. He had never met his employee and he probably never would but he would provide feedback via emails. And in regard to his job, he totally understood the mothers, he was fully behind his employer one hundred percent. If ever needed he would defend her to end of the earth. But the fact was that he never thought it would get to that stage. As far as he was concerned the silent majority would be behind her. The legal system had got too liberal when it allowed recidivists out on the streets to kill, murder, rape, butcher. Something had to be done. He was doing his small bit and he felt good about it. It was never for the money. To see the look on grief torn mother's faces, to see that he was able to bring them a little bit of respite in their darkest hours, that was payment enough.

He got in his car. He had another 3 calls that day.

L.

THE RELEASED PRISONER ON THE PRISON STEPS

As the 'perp' made his way to the exit his mind was filled with exciting thoughts. It had taken 18 years to get to this point. He was going to relish it. No mistakes this time. No getting caught. Hell, prison hadn't' changed him. It had just given him time to become better. Did they really think they could cure people like him. The fools. Was it no wonder that there were so many like him. The sanctions were poultry.

As the doors opened he could not believe what he saw in front of him. He looked around. There was no one else being released, in fact no one else on the pavement so it must have been for him.

There in front of the perp, outside the steel prison doors, was a brand new, gleaming, black, stretched limousine. The longest, blackest and shiniest he had ever seen. Very impressive. The driver's door opened and a monster of a man got out. As the uniformed 6'4' chauffeur approached him he caught his breath. The chauffeur walked up to him and offered his hand for a handshake and politely introduced himself.

Now the perp was cautious. He'd learned the hard way. Lights at the end of the tunnel were normally oncoming trains. He studied the driver, the limo, the circumstances.

'Sir, sorry to surprise you like this. I can understand your shock and we wish we could have done this some other way but my Boss does not like prisons. I am sure you can understand that. My Boss has been monitoring your progress from afar for some time, for 18 years to be exact. It would appear that you both have an awful lot in common and he would like to discuss a mutual solution with you that might deal with, as it were, your enemies,' and that said this he motioned the 'perp' towards the limo.

The perp had learned a long time ago that if something was too good to be true then it normally wasn't. But, he was dropping his guard. He may have thought that 18 years in prison had improved his mind, but at the end of the day it had actually dulled his normal cautious, attentive self.

The 'perp' thought that this definitely beat a 45 minute walk to the train station so happily jumped into the limo when the chauffeur opened the door.

In the car, a member of the HOE Team was ready with the chloroform.

The 'perp' awoke 3 days later in a cage. Incarcerated again but this time with no chance of escape, from anything. Apart from Hell.

M.

THE ESCAPEE

The escapee was asleep on a very comfortable bed compared to what he was used to. What with what he had had to eat, the wine and the 'long run' he was looking forward to a very good night's sleep. The first one in a long time. He had made sure he had a 'weapon' (obtained from the kitchen) beside the bed just in case the occupants returned. He did not want to be be caught out, again. And if they did return, well nothing, absolutely nothing was going to stop him now.

But as much as he expected a pleasant dream at 0400 in the morning he sensed something in his subconscious mind. Something not quite right. Something negative. Something alien. Almost a nightmare. He had had enough rough nights sleep in prison that he always felt that he slept with one eye open. But to some extent, the meal, wine and run had put paid to that.

He awoke suddenly, awakened from a very deep sleep. A gloved hand was placed firmly over his mouth. He tried to speak. He could breath but could not utter a single word. His arms and legs were pinned down. Questions raced through his mind. What the hell had happened? There were 4 men surrounding his bed. His first thought was prison officers. But they certainly did not look like prison officers. They looked like what he would call soldiers, mercenaries, dressed all in black. Who the hell were they? How did they find him? He'd covered all his tracks. There was no way anyone on earth anyone could have followed him. Was this even linked to his escape? Having said that, there was no way they looked 'official'. Questions streamed through his now very awake and conscious mind. One in particular. By the look of these guys they meant serious business. He wasn't going to talk his way out of this one.

He was assessing his situation, quickly. His arms and legs were pinned down to the extent that he could not move. He could not move a muscle nor scream out. All he could move was his eyes.

The commanding officer nodded to her comrades and approached him. Even as she moved there was silence. Their presence and stealth like approach was almost eerie. He felt himself being held even tighter.

She bent down, put her mouth near his ear and spoke to him softly, 'Sorry about this. Hardly the best way to wake up is it? But then again, nothing about this is normal, is it?'

He tried to resist the way in which he was being restrained. She sighed, 'Don't even try. Escape is futile. Don't waste time and effort considering such. If we tracked you this far then you must know, whoever we are, we are serious, almost fanatical some would say.'

She let him digest her words and then continued. 'I suppose you're thinking, who are we, what are we going to do? I don't blame you. Well, look at this way. We are not going to hurt you (she lied). Look upon us as your judge and jury for everything you've done in your miserable, little life that your peers might consider bars your entry into what some might call Heaven.'

Her final words to him and the last thing he heard were the words, 'I said we were not going to hurt you and I meant it. Well, not now anyway. Welcome to the next and last phase in your life............Welcome to Hell on Earth.' And she pointed to the three gold letters on her uniform chest. H O E.

He saw one of the approaching black balaclava officers prepare a syringe and then he felt nothing. It was the last time he would feel nothing.

He awoke 4 days later in a metal container.

N.

THE RESCUE

The kidnapper awoke with a start. Something wasn't right. Something was most seriously wrong. Even before he opened his eyes he knew he was in trouble. He'd been in and around trouble all his life. He'd always felt that the detection of such was his sixth sense. He opened one eye. Blearily he could make out the image of four hooded men standing around his bed. The first thing he noticed was that these were no ordinary men. Their stature, their build, their very presence commanded respect and more importantly from his point of view, obedience. Even before they had said anything he knew he was in trouble. He'd been in unfavourable positions before that were not to his advantage. But this was some serious shit.

However, he was a born criminal and that fighting spirit inside him made him surreptitiously glance at his suitcase under which was his gun. He glanced over at where he had left them. Neither the suitcase nor the gun were there.

The leader of the HOE Team was finally happy. Though thorough professionals, they had still learnt a lot over the last few years. This was a totally different game, but one they fully supported. When a soldier truly believes in what he or she is doing, it can add a tremendous amount of strength to their spirit. This time he and his best team were in time. Most unfortunately they had to let the police deal with the kidnapper's accomplice but they'd get him eventually. The kidnapper was their priority. It's just that they needed those few extra minutes, just in case the accomplice squealed and led the police to this address.

The leader addressed the kidnapper in a commanding tone, 'Now, you don't know me but hopefully you have quickly realised that escape is futile. But well done you, on the one hand kidnapping the richest man on the planet's granddaughter might have seemed like a good idea at the time. After all, if you going to ask for a record ransom then why not. However, unfortunately for you, out of 7.6 billion people on the face of this planet, you most definitely chose the wrong man. And for that, probably for the first time in your life, you are going to pay. Ironic isn't it?'

The kidnapper was thinking fast. One thing in particular worried him. He had grown up and spent all his life with criminals. But these guys looked different. Their dress, their demeanour, their body language, the way the leader spoke, scared the living shit out of him. And he'd met some bad asses in his time,

The one that had spoken to him called out an order. Two more hooded men entered the room. Whilst one of them calmly entered the bedroom next door and checked the health of the young girl another one of the men approached him with a hypodermic syringe in his hand. He could hear the granddaughter being told that she was safe, that they were there at the behest of her grand father, that her ordeal was finally over and she was going home to her mother and grandfather. The officer spoke to the girl. She was crying in relief. For the first time in a few days she finally felt at ease. Particularly as she had seen this man in her grandfather's house many times, she knew him. If he was her grandfather's friend, then she knew she was finally safe, at last.

Another officer was on a mobile phone. 'Yes sir, I am happy to tell you that the mission has been a 100% success. Your granddaughter is healthy, well, unscathed as it were. She knows who we are, that you sent us and that she is safe. Additionally we have the kidnapper, he is alive and kicking for the moment, well maybe not so much kicking if you know what I mean.'

The grandfather asked the HOE Team member a question. He replied, 'Yes sir, he is now due for process'. Those were the last words the kidnapper heard.

He awoke 2 days later on board a container ship, in a cage, strapped to a bed, connected to a machine and there he would lie, uncomfortable some would say, to his natural, dying day and his new life in Hell.

THE END

Printed in Great Britain
by Amazon